PRO....

USA TODAY *Bestselling Author*

PENNY WYLDER

ISBN-13: 978-1727232998

ISBN-10: 1727232992

3

CHAPTER ONE

Ollie

The doorbell rings, and I internally groan. I'm not even sure why I ordered food, I'm too sick to my stomach to eat. And I don't want to see *anyone*. Not even the delivery guy. Closing my eyes, I lean my head back against the couch. Maybe if I ignore him long enough, he'll just leave the food by the door.

I'm in clothes that no one should ever witness me wearing and probably would be better off in the trash: A t-shirt that's so worn it's falling off my shoulders and ratty sweatpants that would never be decent in public because they have more holes than pants. But I didn't want to put on anything nicer. Not after tonight. These are the only clothes worth wearing in my state of mind.

The doorbell rings again.

Just go away, I silently beg him. Leave the mozzarella sticks and milkshake. Leave me to wallow in my self-pity. But he rings the doorbell again, and then my phone starts to buzz. Damn it. Answering the phone is even worse than answering the door. I know it's the just the unfortunate person who's trying to deliver my food, and I cringe.

"Hello?"

"Delivery."

"Yeah," I say, my voice squeaking. "Can you just leave the food by the door?"

There's an uncomfortable pause.

"Sorry, you have to sign the receipt."

"Oh," I say. "Okay, I'll be right there."

Let's get this fucking over with. I keep my blanket wrapped around my shoulders so that my ratty clothes are less visible, and go to the door. The guy is just standing there with my food and I feel even worse for making him wait. "Sorry," I mutter, taking the receipt and not meeting his eyes. I give him a good tip before sealing myself back on the safe side of the door. My goal was no more humiliation for tonight. Missed that shot for a mile.

I suppose it's my own fault though, I didn't have to go on that date. In fact, Lorraine told me that it was a bad idea. But he was cute and I hadn't been on a date in a really long time. I think it's going to be another *very* long time before I risk that again.

8

Sinking back into the couch and my cocoon of pillows, I take a sip of the vanilla milkshake. Sweet bliss. I know that I shouldn't drown my sorrow with sugar and fried cheese, but fuck it, I can go back to being healthy tomorrow.

I'm re-watching one of my favorite TV series—an overly polite British reality show about amateur bakers. I mean, amateur my ass. They may not get paid for their baking but you better believe they're experts. I'm the amateur. I can't make a cake that doesn't come out lopsided. It doesn't mean that I don't try, though.

Stupid moron, I say to myself. I'm not sure whether I'm talking to myself or to Jason, my ill-fated date, but the words fit regardless. I try to lose myself in an episode

9

about making the perfect identical little cakes, but the embarrassment keeps rolling through my head like my brain has the track on repeat.

I thought it had been going well enough. We went to a little Mexican place on the Lower East Side, and it was nice. He was sweet and charming and the conversation was flowing. He works for one of the larger law firms downtown, and even though all of our interests didn't align, enough of them did. In my mind, it was one of the better first dates that I've ever had. Until we walked to the subway.

With an effort, I freeze the tape in my mind. I'd really rather not relive it again, though I know it's only a matter of time.

A text buzzes on my phone, and I glance at the screen. It's Lorraine.

How did it go?

I roll my eyes. Of course she's going to want to know. But she can know later.

A couple of minutes later my phone buzzes again.

Ollie...

I turn the phone upside down on the other end of the couch. It vibrates a couple more times, but I don't look. It's judging time and I want to see how the raspberry mint cakes stack up against the orange cardamom. Even if I already know the answer.

11

There's a knock on the door and I jump. Did the delivery guy forget something?

Then a loud, brassy voice. "Ollie, it's me. Let me in."

Fuck. Lorraine. "Go away!" I want to wallow in my misery, and Lorraine isn't going to let me do that.

There's the sound of a key in the lock and I groan. The door opens and her heels—Lorraine always wears heels—click on my floor. "I should have never given you that key," I say.

"Yes, you should have," she says as she comes around the corner into the living room. She sees me in my nest of blankets and my comfort food. "What the hell happened?"

"I don't want to talk about it."

12

"Too bad."

I defiantly dip another mozzarella stick into my marinara sauce. "What are you doing here?"

She flops down onto the couch next to me, ignoring both my glare and my personal space. "I was on my way home. When you didn't answer my texts, I wanted to see if you were still out or if you were home. And here you are."

"Here I am," I say bitterly, taking a sip of milkshake.

"So what happened?"

The judges on TV think that the orange and cardamom cakes are more successful, since the mint didn't really come through in the cake or the frosting. "I said I don't want to talk about it."

"Too bad."

"Lorraine, please," I say, fighting off a sigh.

She puts her arm around my shoulders. "No. You know why? Because you hold onto these things. You overthink them, and bury them so you're never able to let go. So you're going to tell me about it, and then I'm going to give you some good news."

"Can't you give me the good news now?"

"Nope." She steals a mozzarella stick and bites into it. "I'm holding it hostage for your date story."

I dig through the blankets for the remote and pause the show. Lorraine and I have been friends long enough that I know she's not going to give in. If I don't start talking, she's just going to stare at me until I do. So I start talking. I tell her about the beginning of the date and how cute he was and how it seemed to be going well.

And then I get to the subway.

I take a deep breath. "Well, he was hot. And you know me, I'm not the kind of person that goes home on the first date. But it's been...a while, and I thought, what the hell, let's do it. So we were standing there at the subway, and I was wondering if he was going to kiss me or not, and I asked if he wanted to go back to his place." I shove another mozzarella stick in my mouth.

"And?" Lorraine prods.

"And he *laughed*."

She gasps, "*What?*"

"He laughed, and not like a little laugh. Like a big fucking laugh. Like people on the next block probably heard him crack up."

"Geeze."

I swallow. "And when he was done laughing, he told me that he wasn't looking for some kind of slut, and that even if he was, I wasn't really in is league. And then he asked if I thought that it had really gone that well."

Lorraine blinks. "Well fuck that guy."

I laugh once, but it's not really funny. "Yeah, fuck that guy. Please don't say that you told me so."

"Oh please," she says, "I thought it wasn't a great idea because he looked like a

16

bro not because I thought he was going to be a complete dick."

"Yeah…"

She snuggles against me. "Well, for what it's worth, I'd hoped you weren't answering my texts because you were getting some. And seriously, fuck that guy. I bet he doesn't call himself a slut when he has first-date sex."

"Probably not."

Lorraine sits back up, curling her legs underneath her and facing me. "Now for the good news. It's gonna cheer you up."

"Oh?" I raise an eyebrow.

"Saturday is our ten-year reunion."

I think, and I'm drawing a blank. "For what?"

"For high school."

My jaw drops. "You've got to be kidding me."

She shakes her head. "I'm not."

"Why on earth would you think that that's good news? Or that it would cheer me up?"

"It's not the *reunion* that's going to cheer you up, but one of the people going."

I feel sick to my stomach. If I'd known Lorraine was going to spring some sort of high school surprise on me, I wouldn't have eaten this much cheese. "Do I even want to know?"

"Adam Carlisle."

My stomach drops, and in spite of myself, my pulse jumps up so that it's racing.

"How do you know that?"

She pulls out her phone. "There's a Facebook page for the event. I'm sure they invited you."

"They did," I say, suddenly remembering. "I deleted it."

"I figured. But I did a little stalking. Adam doesn't post to Facebook very much, but he *does* have an Instagram. And god bless the fact that he does."

She shoves the phone in my face, and I understand immediately. Adam was hot in high school. And because he was hot in high school, the fact that he's even hotter now is astonishing. There are several pictures of him at formal events where his suits are perfectly tailored to his body, and then there's some…

other pictures.

Lorraine doesn't hesitate—she blows up a picture of Adam on the beach, diving for a volleyball. He's shirtless, and my mouth is suddenly dry. Adam was an athlete in high school. Basketball. And he had a killer body then. His body now would make his old body hang its head in shame. Even flying through the air in the picture, every line of muscle is visible. He's pure power packed into a sleek package, and I look away.

Even if I'll never admit it, Adam has always been *the* guy. He's the star of every fantasy that I've ever had. And even though I hadn't seen that particular picture, I've definitely looked him up over the years. I'm well aware of how panty-meltingly gorgeous he is. I've had several pairs of panties ruined from thoughts that follow that train. But it's not a good thing. I shouldn't be hung up on a guy from high school that for all I know helped orchestrate the single worst moment of my life. It's not healthy. I should really consider therapy.

"*He's* why you're going to go with me."

I laugh, and this time it's real. "No, I am not."

"Oh come on," she begs, "It'll be fun. Don't you want to see Adam again?"

I do. Oh, I do. I'd love the chance to see him in person. But now, just as every time I've have that thought in the last ten years, bright red embarrassment creeps in and I know that I can't ever face him again. "You know I can't."

"Ollie, all that was ten years ago. People probably don't remember, and if they do…it was high school, so who cares?"

"I care."

"Listen, I think you deserve another chance at your high school crush. Especially when your crush is *this hot*!" She shoves the phone in front of my face for emphasis.

"He wasn't my crush!" I say, probably too quickly. "I just…liked him a little."

Lorraine rolls her eyes. "Girl, you were crushing so hard I thought *my* ovaries were going to explode just by being in your proximity. Yours were already toast."

I shake my head. "That doesn't make it better. The last time I saw him is when… everything happened. How do you move past that?"

"Sasha is a bitch. She's always been a bitch. That's what I'd tell everyone."

"All that's going to do is make me look bad." I shove the blanket off my lap and gather the trash from my food. "I'm not going to go anyway, so it doesn't matter."

Lorraine follows me. "Olllllllieeeeee," she whines, dragging my name out, pleading. "Don't make me go alone. Please? I'll make sure you look so fucking fabulous that no one is going to remember prom night."

"Lor..."

"Please? Please? I swear it will be okay. If anyone says anything to you, I'll punch them in the face, and then no one's going to bother you because they'll all be talking about

23

me. Please?"

She's trying to make me laugh and it works. "You promise?"

"I do. You're going to be so hot, Adam is going to fall over when he sees you." I know that won't happen, but my breath catches and I find myself blushing. Lorraine squeals. "See? I knew you wanted to see him."

"Shut up," I mumble under my breath.

She pulls me back into the living room. "Come on, we'll look at dresses through my portal on the site and tomorrow you can come try them on."

Lorraine is a personal shopper at Bergdorf Goodman, and is undisputedly the best person in her department. Her supervisors know it too. She can't legally tell me, but I know that she dresses her fair share of celebrities that live in New York. So borrowing a couple of dresses for a class reunion? No sweat given the amount of money that she makes for the store.

My job is...far less glamorous. I'm an accountant. Don't get me wrong, I like my job. I like the comfort of numbers and the way I can make them fall in line. And in a city with a whole lot of numbers to make fall in line, I can't complain—I know that I'm a lot better off than many people in this city.

My best friend has already kicked off her shoes and commandeered my laptop, logging into her shopping portal. Part of the time she works from home, prepping what she's going to show her clients with a portal that has live listings of the store's stock.

By the time I sit down with my glass of water, she's already entered in my sizes and is scrolling through pages of dresses. "Aren't reunions usually less formal?" The dresses she's looking at belong on the runway and not in our old high school gym.

"Do you remember high school at all?" Lorraine says, playful sarcasm filling her voice. "Think about who went there. You think there's any chance that *that* group of people is going to plan an event where you can show up in a t-shirt and jeans?"

"I'd be the luckiest person on earth if they did."

She laughs. "No. It's at the Plaza."

"Are you serious?" I shake my head. "Well, at least that's convenient."

"Right?"

I lean back on the couch and let her go to work. She knows what looks good on me better than I do anyway. It's amazing, I didn't want to see anybody, and even though I'm still upset, she's made me feel better. "Thanks, Lor."

"Anytime."

CHAPTER TWO

Ollie

The lights in this mirror are so bright that they're blinding me, but the cheerful blonde girl applying make-up to my face assures me that they're necessary for her to work. Her name is Maren and she works with Lor, who seems to have disappeared for the moment.

I'm sitting in one of the make-up chairs at Bergdorf Goodman, and letting all the stuff that Lorraine has planned unfold. She made me try on about a million dresses and wouldn't let me see how I looked in any of them, and wouldn't tell me which one she picked. If I didn't absolutely trust that she's going to make me look fabulous, I'd be freaking out right now.

Okay, I *am* freaking out right now, but not because of the dress. In an hour I'm going to walk across the street to the Plaza and into a ballroom of former classmates. I'll probably throw up all over the dress Lor's picked. I hope that's within her discretionary budget.

I'm trying to breathe. It must not be working because Maren asks, "Are you all right?"

"Fine." The high pitch of my voice makes it clear that I'm not. "Just nervous."

"Honey, after I'm done with you, you'll have nothing to be nervous about."

"Oh, it's not that," I say. "It's just that the last time I saw all of these people something really… I'm not looking forward to it."

I open my eyes for a second and she nods, understanding. "Well, we'll make sure you look great. You give them hell."

I laugh. "I'll try."

My hair is already done, and the stylist managed to style my hair in a way I always wished it could look but never accomplished myself. It's a simple style, falling in waves down my back with the sides twisted away from my face. I only get a glimpse of myself before she waves my eyes closed again, but Maren knows what she's doing.

She's brushing my face and lining my

lips and I go into a zen-like zone while I let her work. I nearly jump out of my skin when I hear Lorraine's voice. "How are we doing in here?"

"Geeze, Lorraine."

"Sorry," she grins. "Business voice. You look great!"

I glance toward the mirror, and she's right. My eyes look bigger and more green than they usually are. She picked a deep berry color for my lips that I never would have chosen for myself. The effect is amazing. "Thank you," I say to Maren.

"No problem."

Lorraine guides me to dressing rooms. These aren't your typical dressing rooms; they're extra luxurious and usually reserved for the store's A-list clients. "You're going to look so badass," she says, pointing to a room.

Behind the curtain I find an icy blue silk dress, and freeze. "Lor?"

"Yeah?" her voice is muffled across the room in her own alcove.

"What is this?"

I can practically hear her eyes roll. "It's your dress."

"I didn't try anything like this on."

She slides back the curtain already undressed to her underwear and it's my turn to roll my eyes. "No, you didn't try that dress on. But it came in after you'd already left and I knew that it would be perfect. And," she says, holding out a finger before I interrupt, "if you absolutely hate it and want to set yourself on fire, I have a back-up dress. But you're not going to hate it. It's perfect." She slides the curtain shut, and I know that I'm going to lose this fight.

I take a closer look at the dress. It's beautiful. Turning it on the hanger, I see that this dress is backless. The thin beaded straps that I saw from the front fall all the way to the waist of the dress where it catches the drape. Is she crazy?

But I put the dress on. Lorraine has decided she wants to see me in this dress. So I'll show her and tell her I want something different.

I slide back the curtain and walk to one of the pedestals that are framed by three-pane mirrors. And the sight of myself in the dress makes me freeze again.

Damn it. The fact that Lor is so, so right is going to make her day. Her year.

It's not only that it's a gorgeous dress, it's that it's *the* dress. There's a book series that Lor and I loved as teenagers. She's kind of moved on. I haven't. I still love *World's Waterfall* and I re-read it regularly, still hoping that the series will be finished before I'm too old to read it or the author dies. But there's a scene in one of the books—the scene that everyone talks about where the hero and heroine finally get together—and she's wearing a dress that is described a lot like this.

I won't lie, the fact that I look like her is making me freak out inside. There's an excitement building in my chest that I wasn't expecting. Outside, I'm still frozen, standing and looking at myself in the mirror.

Lorraine comes out of her dressing room in her own dress, sees me and breaks into a huge smile. "Oh. My. God. You look fucking fantastic."

"Lorraine, you know that this is *the* dress."

"I know," she grins. "When it came in, I just knew. I *knew* you had to have that dress."

I shake my head, looking back at my reflection. I look like I always imagined the heroine would, beautiful and ethereal. But how can I take this, the way I look and feel, into a situation that's sure to blow up into a massive shit storm? When I say as much to Lorraine, she rolls her eyes.

"Girl, you are wearing that dress. And I believe that the power of that dress will overcome anything bad that could possibly happen. And if people are idiots, I'm going to take you out and we'll paint the town blue with you in that dress because we're not wasting it."

"Okay." I'm not totally convinced, but her enthusiasm makes me want to believe.

I slide into the silver shoes that she put in my dressing room and switch my essentials into my clutch. We're leaving the rest of our stuff here. Lor will get it later. I guess there's not anything else to do except…go to the party.

Lorraine loops her arm in mine and I brace myself. I hope I don't regret this.

CHAPTER THREE

Adam

I'm honestly not sure why I'm here. Sure, the Plaza is beautiful, but there aren't a lot of people from high school that I want to see. A couple, maybe, but this party is way over the top.

The minute I walked into the ballroom I felt out of place. I never felt like I belonged in this crowd of people when I was seventeen, I sure don't feel like I fit in now that everyone has grown up to be richer and more pretentious.

A girl waves at me from across the room. I smile and nod, but I don't remember her. Heading over to the bar, I wait in the line avoiding eye contact with anyone. My father thought it would be a good idea for me to come, show my face to some of my now-famous classmates. Everyone who went to my school is someone now—or at least it feels that way.

"Adam Carlisle!" A hand lands on my shoulder, and I turn to find Trent Bingham—one of the few people I was close with in high school, though we haven't seen each other in years. I'm not going to admit how relieved I am to see a familiar face.

I clap him on the back as well. "Hey, man. How are you?"

"Pretty good," he says as we move forward in the line. "Absolutely hating this. You?"

"Oh, I'm having the time of my life," I deadpan.

He laughs. "Yeah, I thought so. What are you up to now?"

"Medicine," I say.

"You actually did it. Congrats. That's huge! What's your specialty?"

We've reached the bar now, and I order a whiskey. "Pediatrics."

Trent shakes his head, "The women must love you."

I squash down a grimace. "I do all right." I'd rather not talk about that complicated part of my life right now. "What are you doing?"

"Finance. Pretty standard answer in this room I'd imagine."

"Probably," I chuckle, "But it's still a good one." I raise my glass to him, and he cheers as well.

Walking away from the bar, we find a table near the dance floor, which is empty. We're still in the eating and mingling phase of the party.

"I honestly didn't expect to see you here. You were never one for parties."

"No," I shake my head. "You're right. It was suggested I might want to show my face to all the fancy people to make sure my reputation and public profile get a boost." I resist the urge to roll my eyes, but I smile. Trent was one of the guys I could always be real with, and even in the couple minutes we've been back together it feels that way again. He's always had a gift for making people feel comfortable and open, something I imagine comes in handy in the finance world.

"Ah, yes," Trent says, putting on a tone. "So that big investors like me will be impressed by your work in the pediatric field and make a generous donation to your hospital."

"Precisely."

The band starts up a new song, and a memory hits me like a wave—prom night. That was probably one of the strangest nights of my life. There's a commotion by the door and I look over and my whole body goes cold, then hot. Olivia Mitchell is standing in the doorway.

I didn't think I'd ever see her again.

Nobody thought we'd ever see her again. But there she is, alive and… beautiful.

And then she looks right at me. It feels like my heart stops. This song, looking at each other. It feels all too familiar, and I don't think that I can keep still.

I glance over at Trent. "Excuse me."

He follows my gaze and smiles. "It's about time, man. Go."

I leave my whiskey at the table, and I head straight for her. It's like I'm being pulled, and she's looking at me like I'm the last person she expected to see. I hope that I'm not the last person that she wanted to see. Olivia. Ollie. It's been a long time, and there are emotions welling up inside my chest that I haven't examined in a long time.

The first step is to say hello, Adam. Don't get ahead of yourself.

It's shallow, but I'm stunned by how gorgeous she looks. Ollie was always beautiful in a quiet way, but it's not quiet tonight. I try to pull my eyes away from the blue dress hugging her amazing body or else my dick is going to be as hard as granite. But holy fuck do I want to look and never stop looking.

She looks away from me and suddenly I can breathe again. And then I can't, because Sasha is walking up to her.

Shit. I change my course across the ballroom. I'm going to talk to Olivia, I have to, but not while Sasha is there. Not after… everything. I look back and our eyes meet again. Somehow I manage to give her a small smile. I'm bummed I'll have to wait to talk to her, but at least it gives me a chance to figure out what I'm going to say.

I walked into this ballroom dreading this night. Now I'm not sure if there's any place that I'd rather be.

CHAPTER FOUR

Ollie

I was right. I think I'm going to be sick. The air outside Bergdorf's is that rare perfect New York summer. The breeze is cool and you feel magic and possibility in the air. Right. Magic. But I've already seen three people from my high school class walk into the doors in front of us, and I'm not feeling so magical anymore.

Lorraine has a firm grip on my arm, and I know that she's not going to let me fall. It's comforting. And then we're walking inside and I can't breathe. "Ollie," Lor says softly, "chill. You're fine."

She's right. I am fine.

Totally fine.

There's a cluster of people around the entry table with everyone's name tags. I notice a girl in a vibrant yellow dress. Her name is Diana and she was one of the people who was nice to me despite me being a total nerd.

She catches my eye and the does a double-take of recognition. The rest of the group follows her gaze and suddenly I'm being stared at by seven people. It feels like a thousand, and blood rushes to my face. Turning away quickly, I follow Lor—who's already pinning on her name tag—and step up to the table.

"Olivia Mitchell."

The girl sitting behind the table looks

up suddenly, and then I watch as her eyes drift deliberately down to my wrists and back. That's… weird. She shakes her head. "Sorry. Here you go!" The smile she puts on is overly cheerful.

I pin the name tag to the jewel strap of my dress and joy Lor at the edge of the ballroom. "Did you see the way she looked at me?"

"Not everyone is looking at you, Ollie," she rolls her eyes.

The minute she says my name, heads spin. The people standing by the entrance see me, and their eyes go wide. I see people turn and whisper, and the next row turn and whisper. Even with the music, you can hear it, the hushed tones of my arrival being announced. This is what I was afraid of.

"Okay," Lorraine says, "I guess they're looking at you now."

"Thanks, I noticed."

She loops her arm through mine again. "No matter," she says. "We're going in and we're going to be absolutely fucking fabulous!" She says it loud enough that all the people whispering can hear.

Then it happens. The first notes of the song from prom night start to play, and I feel like I'm being pulled into a vortex of sound and memory. Right there, across the room, is Adam Carlisle, and he's looking right at me.

I'm dreaming. I have to be dreaming, right?

My stomach drops into free-fall. He looks amazed, shocked, but not unhappy. I

know that I'm dreaming now. And then he
gets up and starts walking toward me.

Lorraine sees him too. "Did I tell you
or did I tell you? Girl."

"He's not coming over to talk to me," I
say. But I can tell that he is. I just can't believe
it.

He's looking at me. *At* me. Like I'm the
only thing he sees, and every feeling that I had
in high school comes rushing back. Lor was
absolutely right. I had the biggest crush on
him. I was utterly in love with him, and I
might still be, just a little bit.

How can this be happening right now?
Maybe everything is magic tonight: this dress,
the weather outside, Adam. But then again,
everything once seemed magical before. And

then it all went wrong, and there's nothing
that can ever change that.

CHAPTER FIVE

Ollie

Senior Year

The sound of bouncing basketballs is echoing loudly in my ears, but I don't mind. I'll sit through it if I have to in order to watch Adam. If Lorraine were here, she'd roll her eyes, but I can't get enough of watching the way he moves. Every move is so confident and smooth, and I wish I were more like that.

The game is in full swing, and even though this isn't my normal scene, I find myself enjoying it. Though it's fair to say that I don't think that I'd be enjoying basketball as much without my particular brand of eye-candy. I don't really know when my crush on Adam started, only that it's been growing more and more out of control. I see him when I watch movies and read books. When my eyes close, I imagine him kissing me. I dream about it too.

I imagine him catching me as he's leaving school and pulling me around the building to the area where the old trees cast shade and beautiful patterns on the brick walls of the courtyard. He shares a smile with me—like we're both in on a secret—and puts a finger to his lips. We wait, hidden together while the school empties, and his fingers slowly curl around mine.

"I've wanted to do this for a while," Adam says.

I pretend that I don't know what he's talking about. "What?"

He doesn't say anything. Instead, he tilts my chin up and closes the distance between us. I close my eyes as his lips touch mine, and I feel like I'm flying and falling and shaking and that I'll never be the same. It's perfect, and I never want it to—

I jump as soda splashes down onto my head and onto my copy of *World's Waterfall*.

"Oh my god, I am *so sorry*." An overly sweet voice says. Sasha Green sits down next to me and dabs at the book and my hair with her napkin. She's still in her jazz dance costume from half time, and she's looking at me with concern. "Are you okay? I must have slipped."

That's odd, because it's a fact that Sasha is the best dancer in the school. She doesn't slip. But I nod. After being startled out of that particular fantasy, I don't really want to talk to anyone. But she doesn't move on. Instead she sits next to me and pulls the book out of my hands. "What are you reading?"

I don't have the chance to answer because she turns the book over and scans the back, and I can already see her face pulling into a grimace. The crowd around us cheers and I look toward the court to see Adam jogging away from the basket with a smile on his face. He scored.

"Wow, that's a big smile," Sasha says cheerfully. I hadn't realized I was smiling at him, and I make sure to make my face go blank. "Aww, it's okay," she says, putting the book back into my lap. "You like him."

"He's a nice guy," I say, still hoping that she'll go away. But Sasha Green isn't a person that you ask to go away. Doing that just means you'll be the target of the popular crowd for a month.

She shakes her head. "That's not what I mean. I mean that you *like him* like him."

"No, I don't."

"It's okay if you do," she says sweetly. "It's cute."

I try to shake my head, to form the words to stop this. The last thing I need is for it to get back to Adam that I have a crush on him. I would die. Actually and literally die. "It's not like that."

Sasha tilts her head. "That's too bad.

There's nothing wrong with liking someone.
How do you think Adam would feel if he
knew that you *don't* like him?"

My face flushes, and my body goes hot.
I can feel myself start to panic, and I know
that I need to leave. I'm not sure how she's
managed to do it—turn my words back on me
twice—but it's safer if I leave. "I—I have to
go."

"So soon?" She gives me a smile that
looks friendly on the surface.

I grab my bag off the bleachers and
edge my way past some people to the stairs.
The game is close to the end and people are
so caught up in it that they don't even notice
me going by. As soon as I'm away from Sasha,
I feel a little better. I don't know what that
was about, but I don't like it. Bad things

56

happen when people like Sasha pay attention to people like me.

I look back, and Sasha is still watching me with a sickly sweet smile. She waves, and I speed up, wanting to get out of her orbit as quickly as possible. The world spins and suddenly I'm falling, my bag and books slip and I slam face first into the gym floor.

There's a collective gasp, and I don't move. Everything hurts, but I'm not sure that it hurts more than the fact that I *know* everyone in the gym is looking at me. I can feel blood coming from my nose—I should get up. Get some ice. Hide for the rest of eternity. This is a good to-do list.

I start to push myself up, and suddenly there's a hand grasping my arm, helping me to stand. I'm blushing bright red, but I know I have to thank whoever it is. But my mouth is dry and suddenly I'm shaking. It's Adam.

He looks concerned, actual and real concern and oh my god I can't believe he's seeing me like this. I press my hand to my nose to try to stop the blood, but it's already over. There are tears welling in my eyes and I try to blink them away because I don't want him to see me cry too.

"Are you all right?" he asks.

"I…I don't know." I'm very much not all right. I'll never be able to show my face in school again.

Suddenly I hear footsteps running toward me. "Ollie!" It's Lorraine, coming from across the gym where the cheerleaders are sitting.

Adam leans down and gathers my things. He puts my books and pens back in my bag and gently puts the bag back on my shoulder. I can't move as he does it. Then he hands me my now soda-stained and bloody copy of *World's Waterfall*. He gives me a small smile. "Do you like it?"

I'm a little star-struck. Adam Carlisle helped me. He's so close to me. "What?"

"The book."

"Oh," I say as Lorraine arrives next to me. "Yeah, I do."

"I hope you get the chance to finish it soon."

I can only nod, and he smiles again as Lorraine takes my arm and leads me away towards the doors and the nurse. The mistake

I make is looking back, and noticing how the whole school is watching me walk away with blood down my face and shirt. By the time we're outside the doors of the gym, I can't hold back the tears anymore, but Lor doesn't stop to comfort me, guiding me straight to the nurse's office. Then she pulls me into a hug. "It's okay."

"It's really, *really* not," I say. "Sasha was already up to something, and this is only going to give her more fuel. People are going to stare at me for weeks, and Adam—" I hiccup, and flinch as the nurse is cleaning up my nose, seeing if it's broken. "Adam probably thinks I'm a total spaz now. He's seen me bloody and crying. That's really sexy."

Lorraine rolls her eyes. "Girl, I love you but sometimes you're stupid as hell."

The nurse gives her a look, and I'm staring at my best friend in shock. "I'm sorry?"

"Didn't you see what Adam did?"

I wince as the nurse puts some antiseptic on the scratches. "No, I was a little busy flat on my face in front of the whole school."

"We were about to win. Adam had the ball and was about to score, and then you fell. He dropped the ball and *ran off the court* when you fell. The game didn't stop, the other team took the ball and scored and we lost."

I think my heart stops in my chest. "What?"

"Adam threw the game to help you. So if you think that he cares about the blood on your face, you need to get your head on straight."

My heart is pounding now. Lorraine has no reason to lie about that. But if it is true, what does it mean?

CHAPTER SIX

Ollie

<u>**Present Day**</u>

Like being conjured out of that
memory, Sasha suddenly appears in front of
me, a giant smile on her face. "Hi!" She wraps
me in a giant hug that I absolutely do not
want to be a part of and I hold my breath
until she lets me go.

Lorraine is staring at her like she's an
absolute idiot, and even though I'm
uncomfortable, I have to try hard not to

laugh. That day on the basketball court was not the only, or even the worst, thing that Sasha did to me. There was the time she accidentally ruined my work in art class, got me blamed for a low score on a group project that was entirely her fault, started multiple rumors about me that resulted in more than one horrifying lunch hour, and of course, prom. And those are just the ones that are coming to mind now.

"Oh. My. God," Sasha says. "I love your dress."

Lor steps closer. "It's Marchesa."

"Well it's working on you." She smiles again. "How are you? I've missed you. It's been so long!"

There's a phantom pain in my nose,

and I touch the bridge of it, remembering that day in the gym. It has been so long, but I sure as hell haven't missed her. But I don't get the same vibe from her that I got in high school. She seems more genuine, like she's actually excited about being here. "Good to see you, Sasha."

She waves to someone across the room. "I have to go say to hi to Corey, but I totally want to catch up! I'll swing back around." She blows us a kiss and floats away toward a group of girls that look like they might be from her old clique.

"Fake bitch," Lor says with an eye-roll.

"I don't know. She seemed a lot more genuine. I suppose it's possible that in the last ten years she's changed."

Lor shakes her head. "Girls like Sasha don't change. They think the world is something they can manipulate, and they never stop trying to do it."

"Maybe." I like to believe that people can change. That people do change. If not, that's just kind of depressing. Now that I'm here, I need a drink. I definitely need a drink. I point to the bar, and Lor nods. I'll find her once I've waited in line and have something that's going to dull my senses a little bit.

Luckily the line isn't too long right now —the Plaza bartenders are on top of it.

"Olivia."

I turn, and my feet drop through the floor. It's Adam. Adam is here, so close to me, and that same memory from the gym overwhelms me. That's the last time we were this close. I can't help how breathless I sound. "Hi."

"Hi." Then he grins. "I'm really glad you came. Honestly I didn't think you would."

"Yeah. I wasn't planning on it. Lorraine convinced me."

"Good thing she did."

My body lights up with joy because he wanted to see *me*. But then I go cold. Is he making fun of me? Is this some kind of joke with Sasha? If Lorraine is right and people like Sasha never change, then what if Adam is the same too? What if it's all another cruel joke?

"How have you been?" he asks quietly, and he glances down toward my hands. I stretch my fingers and the bracelet Lor gave me jingles. Probably just distracted by it.

I nod. "Pretty good. I was…very nervous about coming here."

"Why?"

I laugh. "You really have to ask that?"

"I suppose not."

"I have a life I really like," I say, word vomit spilling out of me before I can stop it. "I moved on from all of this, so I wasn't sure that I wanted to bring that back into my life."

"I get that," he says, and for a second we're quiet. I move forward a place in line and Adam moves with me, hands in his pockets. "Listen, I—"

"ADAM!" There are whoops and hollers and I stumble out of the way as we're swarmed by four members of what used to be the basketball team. A bunch of guys surround Adam, giving him overly amped up hugs and clapping him on the back. He looks as startled as I do, and I wish we hadn't been interrupted. I wanted to hear what he has to say.

Adam glances at me apologetically, and says hello to his friends. It's at that moment that they all decide to notice that I'm standing there. "Damn, Olivia!" It's coming from a guy whose name I think is Brandon. "You got hot."

"Yeah, when did that happen?" Another guy asks. "I'd be happy to take you home and—"

"Okay." Adam interrupts.

Oh my god. Oh my god I can't win. I have guys telling me I'm not attractive enough to spend the night with and then I have assholes telling me how fuckable I am because I have a pretty face.

"Come with us," Brandon says. "We trying to get the Plaza to set up a hoop at that end of the ballroom and get the band back together."

A third from the group puts his hand on Adam's shoulder and tries to guide him away, but he shrugs the hand off. "No thanks, guys. I'm in the middle of a conversation. I'll catch up with you later."

"Seriously?" guy number three asks. Jason, maybe? And then he whispers far too loudly for me not to hear. "I mean, I know she's hot, but it's Olivia Mitchell."

I feel myself flush red, and I watch Adam's face go white with anger. "Fuck off, man."

The guy backs up, hands raised in surrender. "Whatever. Come find us when you want some fun." He looks me up and down, and I feel sick, the look on his face somehow conveying want and disgust at the same time.

"Go," Adam says, and they leave. One of them nearly trips over a chair. It's possible that they might be drunk already. "Are you all right?"

Again, I'm having déjà vu. He said those same words to me that day in the gym. I couldn't believe that he intervened for me then, and I'm honestly having a hard time believing that he did it just now. It seems like

71

way too good to be true.

"I guess so," I say. "Thank you for doing that. It was uncomfortable."

"No kidding." He shakes his head.

Finally up to the bar, I order a glass of wine. When I turn around, Adam is right there, so close. Closer than he was standing just a second ago. He reaches out and takes my hand. "I'd like to talk to you, if that's all right. About that night and some other stuff. But I'd like to do it where we won't be interrupted again."

My heart is pounding in my chest, and I'm not sure that I can breathe or speak right now so I just nod. He looks down again, holding up my hands and sweeping his thumb across my wrists. "Thank you."

I'm not sure about the wrist thing. Maybe he's developed a wrist fetish in the last ten years, but honestly I've heard of weirder stuff and there's nothing at all in this moment that's going to stop me from saying yes.

Adam guides me toward the door and that perfect summer air. From across the room I see Lorraine's jaw drop open. I manage to send her a tiny wave before we disappear out of the ballroom through a balloon arch that's way too similar to the one that was at prom. The last time I saw Adam.

CHAPTER SEVEN

Ollie

Prom Night

"Tighter." Lorraine pushes out all the air in her lungs, and I try to pull the laces of her corset tighter.

"I really think that's it," I say.

She sighs. "Fine, I suppose that's good." She reaches insider the top edge of the crimson corset and adjusts her boobs so that they're practically falling out of it.

I look at myself in the mirror. The dress I ended up choosing is purple, and it's pretty much the opposite of Lorraine's. Mine has a lacy collar around the neck and no cleavage. It's floor length too. I really love the way this dress looks, but I don't want the attention that Lorraine does. I didn't even want to come, really. My nose is still healing from the last event I attended with the whole school.

"Ollie, relax. Try to have fun."

"I will."

"You could dance with Adam."

I immediately flush bright red, "That's not going to happen."

"Fine. But I'm still saying that you could." She smirks at me in the mirror. "I promise that we can dance with each other later. Just as soon as I finish dancing with Joey

Lancaster. He's going to notice how fucking sexy I look tonight." Those last words are more for her than for me.

"I'll hold you to it," I say.

"Perfect," she says, sweeping out the door. "Wish me luck!"

"Luck," I say softly even though she's already gone. I run some water over my hands, hesitating. All night people have been asking me how my nose is. If they were just asking me how I'm doing it would be fine. It's the laughter after they ask that gets me. But Lorraine is right, if I'm already here, I might as well try to go out and enjoy it.

The hallway of the school is dark, and I can hear the music thumping in the gym as I head down the hall. Sasha is in the doorway and I don't know if I've ever seen her look so pissed. I'm thinking about ducking back down the hallway when she spots me. Instantly her entire face changes. "Hi, Ollie!"

I don't know if I've ever heard Sasha say my name before, but it sounds strange. Only people who know me really well call me Ollie. Finishing the length of hallway before I reach the door feels like it takes forever. I'm kind of hoping that I can just go inside and she doesn't want to talk to me, but of course I don't have that kind of luck.

She holds something out to me. "Will you sign my yearbook?"

"Uh, now?"

"Of course! When will there be another time with so many of the

77

upperclassmen in one place?"

She has a point, and I take the book
and pen from her. Snow days and unexpected
repairs to part of the gym pushed our prom
back a bit. We're almost done with classes and
everybody's gotten their yearbooks. I flip to
my senior portrait and go to write something,
but the pen is sticky. Glancing down at my
hand, I see that my fingers are now stained
with glittery blue dye. I go ahead and start
writing. 'Happy graduation, wishing you the
best.'

"By the way, your pen is leaking," I say,
holding up my hand.

She grabs it and looks closer at my
fingers. "Oh god, I'm sorry!"

"It's okay." I pull my wrist out of her

grasp. Suddenly Lorraine appears at my side and she's tugging on my arm. "Dance with me!"

I wave bye to Sasha as I'm pulled into the crowd of dancers. "You looked like you could use a rescue," she says.

"Thank you."

"No problem. Now I'm going back to dance by Joey."

She dances away from me and I slip back out of the dancers, keeping an eye out for Sasha so that she doesn't see that I'm not dancing. I take up a post near the refreshment table and get myself some punch. It's not lost on me that I'm quite the cliché. But I can't say that I'm not enjoying it.

I watch from the sidelines as Lorraine

finally does get her chance to dance with Joey. The look of sheer joy on her face is one that I will never forget. A couple of times I think that I'm about to be asked to dance, but it's never me. That's fine, I like watching everyone. I like seeing the connections form and break and come back together.

And of course, I watch Adam. He dances with a few girls, but also spends a good amount of time on the sidelines. He doesn't seem like he's quite comfortable, and I totally get it. I'm not comfortable either.

Later in the night the music stops, and the librarian Mrs. Marsden takes the stage. "It's about that time everybody! Time for us to find out who's King and Queen of the prom." She waves two white envelopes in the air. "First, our King."

She tears open the envelope and pulls out a piece of paper. Immediately she breaks into a wide smile. "Adam Carlisle!"

The gym bursts into cheers, and I join them. It's not surprising to me at all that Adam is prom king. He's gorgeous and the star of the basketball team, and tonight the tuxedo that he's wearing makes me feel faint, the same way they say that Victorian ladies swoon. I wish that I could be the one standing up with him, the one that gets to dance with him. But that won't happen, because I don't even think half the people in this room know that I'm here. Adam certainly doesn't.

He makes his way to the stage and gets crowned. His smile lights up the room and he waves to the crowd in a mock gesture of a king to his kingdom, and everybody laughs.

"And now for the queen." She tears open the second envelope, but she doesn't break into a smile this time. Instead she looks confused. "Well, this is a surprise. Olivia Mitchell!"

I freeze. *What?*

The entire gym goes silent, so that all you can hear is the pop song in the background. And then the whispers start, and people looking around for me. Oh god. Someone spots me and a path forms between the stage and me . Adam looks confused, and a spike of pain goes through my chest. I mean, I never expected to be voted queen, but the fact that he thinks I couldn't or shouldn't be…hurts.

Someone next to me whispers, "Olivia, go."

I find myself walking slowly towards the stage even though I can't feel my feet. This can't possibly be right, can it? Did my wish that I could dance with Adam as his queen somehow reach the universe? I look around and everyone seems as confused as I am. They're staring and whispering, and I think I might be sick.

But then I look at Adam again, and he smiles. It's a miracle, and I find myself smiling back. Because if this is true, it's everything I've ever wanted and the best moment of my life. Stepping onto the stage, I cross to Mrs. Marsden, who puts the silver tiara on my head. "Everyone give it up for our King and Queen, Adam and Olivia!" There's half-hearted clapping from the crowd. "They'll now have their first dance."

Adam takes my hand and I can't breathe. "Ready to dance?" he asks softly.

"Yeah."

We move off of the stage and into the middle of the dance floor where everyone has formed a circle, and we're in the center spotlight. I can't believe this is actually happening. Adam pulls me close, puts a hand on my waist, and if I wasn't sure that I would kill myself for missing this moment, I think I would faint.

"Stop!" An angry voice comes from across the gym, and then Sasha barges into the circle followed closely by Mr. Andrews, another of the chaperones. She's looking straight at me, and I recognize that same burning anger I saw in the hallway earlier. "Olivia Mitchell is *not* prom queen."

I just blink at her. "What?"

"She cheated. She switched her name in the envelope. It's supposed to be me."

Still on stage, Mrs. Marsden clears her throat into the microphone. "That's a serious accusation, Sasha. Do you have proof?"

Sasha scoffs, walking over to the stage. "Of course I do. Look at the way the name on that paper is written. That blue ink."

"What about it?"

The way she's looking at me, now I know how a bug feels that's about to be stepped on. "I saw her coming from the hallway near the offices earlier, and I saw something else." She comes to me and rips my hand out of Adam's, holding it up for people to see. Suddenly I understand and I'm

85

lightheaded. I really do think I might pass out. The blue ink is still on my fingers from when I signed her book. Lorraine pulled me onto the dance floor and I didn't go back to the bathroom to wash it off. She set me up.

"See?" Sasha says, a smug smile on her face. "She wrote her name herself."

Mr. Andrews looks uncomfortable, but he steps forward. "I'm sorry, Olivia, but I wrote Sasha's name myself, and I did it in black ink."

"It's not true," I say.

"What was that?" She asks.

I swallow, trying to hold myself together. I'm flushed and shaking and I can feel tears dangerously close. This isn't the way this is supposed to happen. "It's not true. You asked me to sign your yearbook with that pen." I look at Mr. Andrews. "Look at her yearbook. You'll see that I'm right."

He doesn't have the chance to respond because Sasha starts laughing. A bold, loud laugh that fills the gym. I see small smiles cracking on people's faces, some of them covering them with their hands. She's winning them over. "Isn't that cute? Everyone in the school knows that you're in love with Adam. It makes perfect sense that you'd do anything you possibly could do dance with him."

I don't dare look back at him. Not now. I don't want to know. "I wouldn't. I wouldn't do this," I say. I look at people in the crowd. I look at the teachers. "I didn't even want to come to prom," I said. "I came with a friend. I didn't…" I trail off because there's not one person who seems to believe me. "How does Sasha even know that my name was written in blue ink? How would she know that if she hadn't seen the envelope herself?"

Just for a second, I think I'm making progress. I see some people try to think about that, but Sasha doesn't let them finish the thought. "Ollie, you're nothing but a cheater. I mean, I understand *why* you did it," she sounds sympathetic, but she's really not, "but it's pathetic." She rips the tiara off my head, and I wince as it tears at my hair. "I think it's time for you to go."

"But—"

"CHEATER!" she yells it in my face.

I try to say something. It's not true. "I'm not—"

"CHEATER!"

A tear slips out, and I can't breathe. She's not going to let me talk or defend myself. She put this together so perfectly that no one is going to question her. "Please," I say, but no one hears it. Sasha is chanting the word now, and other people have joined her. There's pain in my chest, and I can't…I can't…

I look back at Adam, and he looks disappointed. Like he doesn't know what to think of me, and I feel my heart fracture in two. I run, and the crowd parts for me. I'm not sure how I make it to the doors, because I can't see anything.

I've never felt this kind of pain before and I don't know what to do. Somehow I make it to my car, and I collapse into the backseat, letting tears and pain consume me. What did I ever do to make people want to treat me like this? Why couldn't Sasha just leave me alone?

If I never see any of these people again, it'll be too soon.

CHAPTER EIGHT

Ollie

Present Day

The air is still perfect, and Adam doesn't let go of my hand until we're outside and across the street to the square with trees and a fountain by the Plaza. It's a strange kind of place, dark in the middle of New York's brilliance. Somehow all the noise doesn't seem to reach right here, and it feel like we're completely alone.

"How have you been, really?"

I shrug. "I'm fine."

"Are you sure?"

"Yeah," I make a face. "Why?"

Adam scratches the back of his neck, "I was worried about you."

I'm still not getting it. "But why?"

"It's really good to see you," he says. "I'm glad that you're doing well."

"Yeah."

He puts his hands in his pockets. "So what did you decide to do after high school?"

"College," I say. Then I laugh. "I'm kidding. I did go to college, but I'm an accountant now. Super sexy, I know."

"That's great," he says. "Seriously. I would be lost without my accountant. They get a bad rap but I think most people would fall apart without people who actually understand tax law."

"I do get a lot of very nice thank you gifts around tax season."

He laughs. "Anything else? Are you seeing anyone?"

There's no way in hell I'm going to tell him about my nerdy single existence. The life that's not glamorous like tonight. The one where I stay home reading books and watching Netflix and occasionally going on dates with men who don't find me attractive. "Well, that's not fair," I say. "Don't I get to hear about your career too?"

Adam looks suddenly shy. "I'm finishing up the last year of my residency, I graduate next year."

"Residency as in doctor? Wow!"

"You seem surprised," he says, chuckling.

"I mean, I am a little. I guess I figured you'd have gone into finance or something."

He nods. "A lot of guys from our class did. I didn't even really know it was something I wanted to do until college. In fact, I was sure I *didn't* want to be a doctor since both my parents are. But I took a bunch of classes in different fields my first semester, and to make my family happy, one of them was a pre-med bio class. I was surprised how much I loved it. And of course my parents were thrilled. I never looked back."

"That's really great, Adam. What's your specialty?"

"Pediatrics."

Wow. "That's really amazing, Adam." And I mean it. "Where are you?"

"Columbia. I'm hoping to stay there too."

"Good to know that you're not planning to leave anytime soon."

"Why is that good?" he asks with a smile.

I shrug. "No reason. But I do think it's great that you're doing something to help people. I mean, as much as I like my job, I can't really say that."

"Well—"

I hold up my hand. "You know what I mean."

"I do." Adam looks down at the ground, and over at the fountain, then back at me. "I've been thinking about you, Ollie."

I try to ignore the way my breath catches in my chest. "Probably just the reunion. I imagine you've been thinking about everybody in our class."

"No. I've been thinking about you for a long time. I actually never stopped."

I freeze, try to push down the hope that blooms through me. He doesn't mean what I think he means. The only reason that he thought about me was because of everything that happened.

There's a silence for a moment and then he takes a step forward. "I want to apologize."

The intensity in his face is mesmerizing, and I don't want to look away, but I don't understand. "Adam, we haven't seen each other in ten years. What are you apologizing for?"

"For ten years ago. I never got to know you in school the way I really wanted to, and what happened at prom, I shouldn't have just stood there. I should have said something or gone after you. That was my fault."

I close my eyes, fighting against the memory that wells up in my brain, still impossibly painful after all this time. "It wasn't your fault. That was all Sasha."

"No," he says. "I'm the reason that she did it. She wanted me to go out with her, and I turned her down that night."

I open my eyes, and I'm staring into his perfect green eyes and I'm suddenly nervous. What does this mean? "Why did you turn her down?"

"Because I liked you. And she hated that."

Suddenly the question I've been asking myself for ten years—why would Sasha Daniels target me like that—has an answer. I'm not sure if I'm angry or relieved, but I'm glad that I know. If I had known this a long time ago, things would have been different. "I wish you'd told me that a long time ago."

"Yeah," he says. "But you didn't come back, and after that night I didn't think that you'd want to see anyone. And the more time passed the harder it got to consider reaching out. Which is why I'm apologizing now. I should have done more, and I regret not getting to know you when I had the chance."

The words are out of my mouth before I can stop them. "You still can."

It settles in my gut, that I forgive him. It's not his fault that Sasha chose to take his rejection out on me, and yeah he could have done something, could have said something, but he wasn't the only person that didn't. I mean, I wish that he had told me about his feelings a long time ago, but I didn't tell him that I liked him either. And staying angry about it isn't going to help either of us. Besides, maybe there's a chance now.

Adam's face goes still in shock at my words. I don't think he was expecting me to say that. It's fair, I wasn't expecting me to say that either. Yeah, that was probably stupid. He didn't bring me out here to hit on me, he brought me out here to absolve ten years of guilt. The realization of just how wrong I was about this situation creeps up and I blush, embarrassment making me flash hot. "I should go," I say, turning and heading back toward the hotel.

"Ollie, wait," he says. "Don't go."

He manages to grab my hand, and I lose my balance, slipping backwards. He catches me, pulling me upright and against him, and I still can't breathe and now it's for an entirely different reason. Adam has his arms around me, hands against the bare skin of my back and I feel like I'm back in high school because it's all I've ever wanted.

Being pressed up against him, I feel the body that I saw in that photo through his clothes. Hard and strong and absolutely overwhelming. It's not only his muscles that are hard right now, and... oh my god. It's because of me. It really shouldn't take a man's hard-on to be convinced that he wants me, but it suddenly clicks.

I feel like I've got emotional whiplash from the last three minutes.

"You okay?" His voice is lower, rougher than before.

I look up into his face and we're so close now. "Yeah," I say. And I mean it. I'm okay. I can't believe that this is happening. Is it going to happen? I don't know. I don't want to force it. I don't think that I could take that rejection. "You can let me go now."

"Why would I ever do that?"

He leans down and presses his lips against mine and oh...

My whole body feels like champagne, light and bubbly and drunk and it's barely a kiss. I gasp when he pulls back. Our mouths were closed and it was nothing more than lips and I still feel like I've run a marathon—breathless and filled with endorphins and just happy.

His hands roam up and down my back, and I'm very aware of the fact that I'm not wearing any underwear under this dress. I can feel my nipples harden against the silk, and I wonder if he can feel them too. I don't know what to say right now. What do you say in this moment? Where the barest of kisses is better than you ever thought that it could be?

I'm saved from answering that question

because we're both staring at each other, and I can feel the smile on my face. It matches the one that's on his that's making me feel like the sun is shining at midnight in Manhattan.

"May I kiss you again?"

"Please do."

He chuckles as he closes the distance, and this time it's not just lips. His tongue is there, gently asking permission and I open for him, and everything feels like it expands. This is so much more than I thought, so much better. I feel like I'm flying, joy and air and pleasure filling me up until I can't contain it and I kiss him back.

I wrap my arms around his neck and try to pull him closer. I've never had a first kiss like this. I guess it's technically a second kiss. Who cares, I'm kissing Adam Carlisle! My body heats up as our tongues dance and I think I could stay in this moment forever.

I have to catch my breath when we separate. He's stolen all my breath from me. I'd happily let him do it again. "Wow." Is the only word I can say.

He chuckles softly. "I wasn't expecting that." His fingers tighten on my spine. "I didn't want you to run. I was just surprised and wasn't expecting you to forgive me or willing to be near me."

"Better late than never. I've thought about you too. I actually have a confession to make."

"Oh?" he smiles. "Are you keeping a dark secret?"

I laugh. "Not dark, no. I wasn't going to come. I was convinced that I never wanted to see any of our class again. But Lorraine knows me too well—she knows that I never really got over my crush."

"On me?" He's grinning like I've just said I think unicorns are real.

"Yeah, on *you*." I'm glad it's dim here under these trees because I'm blushing again. "I had said no, and then she showed me your pictures. Once I saw them, I realized that you were the only person that I wanted to see. Even if it was only from across the room."

"This is much better than from across the room," he says, and then he kisses me again.

My heart is going to pound itself out

of my chest. God, I'll never be able to thank Lorraine enough for forcing me to come to this reunion. If I had known that this would happen, I never would have fought her on it. I need to buy her the biggest box of her favorite chocolate that I can find.

The energy of this kiss shifts, and I can feel it turn hungry in both of us. I slide my hands inside the jacket of his tuxedo, feeling more of his body, and I'm acutely aware of the fact that his hand is sliding down my back to the low dip of my dress. A few more inches and he's about to realize that there's absolutely nothing separating him from my skin.

I hear the click of high heels a second before I hear her voice. "Ollie?"

Lorraine comes around the corner of

the path and I try to jump back from Adam, unsuccessfully. He doesn't let me go, and we're still entwined together. Adam raises an eyebrow. "Embarrassed?"

"No," I say, blushing. "Though I love getting caught mid-make-out by my best friend." He chuckles, and I turn to face Lor. "Hi."

She smirks. "Hi. I came to get you to dance! The party is finally going, and it's really fun." She looks Adam up and down. "You should come too."

"I'll be right there," I say.

"Sure," she says.

"How did you find us?"

"I followed the sound of your ovaries screaming in ecstasy."

107

"Lor!" I flush bright red as Adam bursts out laughing.

She waves a hand. "Kidding. The doorman said he saw you guys come this way when I described you."

"Okay then," I say. "Bye."

"See you!"

She flounces off, and I turn back to Adam, hiding my face in his shirt. "Now I'm embarrassed."

"Don't be," he says, still laughing a little. "If my best friend were here it might have been worse."

"Is he here?" I ask, not wanting to walk into that particular situation.

Adam shakes his head. "No, he's a friend from med school. I'm sure you'll meet him at some point."

"I'd like to, but I'm glad I don't have to worry about something more embarrassing than that."

He tilts his head to the side. "I think I'd risk it so I could do this again."

There's something in the way that he kisses me that makes New York fall away. I'm standing in the middle of the sky with Adam, nothing exists but the two of us, and I'm prepared for it to stay that way. He pulls away too soon. "Will you dance with me?"

"Hell yeah."

Taking my hand in his again, we walk back into the hotel together, and I ignore the pointedly amused look that the doorman gives us when we pass. God knows what Lorraine said to him when she came back inside.

Lor wasn't kidding, the ballroom is an entirely different place when we walk into it. The lights are low now, with roving streaks of colored light highlighting the dance floor, and it seems more like a club than a ballroom. The benefit of that is no one even notices that Adam and I walk in hand in hand. There's a crush of people on the dance floor and Lorraine is right in the center.

Dancing has never been my thing, but I'll do it for Lor. And the thought of dancing with Adam leads me to dirty places in my mind. Places I definitely shouldn't be dwelling on in public. "Ready?" he asks.

I nod and he pulls me into the crowd, helping maneuver us to where Lor is already completely one with the music. Her smile is brilliant, and she cheers when we reach her, pulling me into a hug and then spinning me back to Adam. "I don't know how to do this!" I shout at him so he can hear me.

"Don't worry," he shouts back, and then he leans down so his voice is in my ear. "I've got you."

Grabbing my hand, he spins me out and pulls me back so that my back is against his chest. The way he's moving with the rhythm is smooth and easy, and his confidence makes it feel easy for me too. One of his hands holds mine, and the other is wrapped around my waist, holding us close so that we move together.

I like the way I can feel the fabric of his clothes against the bare skin of my back, and I like the way his fingers spread across my stomach, confident and a little possessive. I can feel that he's still hard, and the thought that he's hard because of *me* makes my heart beat faster.

Adam's lips find my neck and god I'm glad that it's so loud because I moan. His mouth feels like fire and pleasure and now I'm wondering what his lips will feel like everywhere. *Everywhere.* His hand slips lower on my dress, and it's like every little inch of me he touches is shooting need straight into my gut. I'm going to get lost and forget where I am.

"Adam," I say, but my voice is lost in the music. I turn to face him, and our movement takes on an entirely different feeling. Face to face, hips locked together, and I'm so aroused now that I can't really move.

He's the one who's moving both of us.

I lean forward to whisper in his ear, "I don't want to stop."

"We don't have to."

"If we don't," I say, "I'm going to have a moment more embarrassing than prom."

I watch his eyes go dark and everything about him hardens more, and he holds me more tightly against his body. It doesn't help the problem. The music changes then, to a slower song, and it's like high school all over again. People who haven't paired off suddenly do, and Adam and I blend in perfectly with the other couples. I glance to my left and see Lorraine with Joey Lancaster—honestly I should have seen that coming.

Adam's hand falls on my lower back,

and he takes my other hand in the traditional waltz pose. "I wanted to dance with you that night, you know."

"Did you?"

"I was as surprised as you were that night, and when it seemed like you had won, it was too perfect. But I should have realized something was wrong earlier. I had just told Sasha that I liked you. But I was so happy…" Adam looks embarrassed now. "I'm glad I have the chance to do this now."

"Sorry I'm not a better dancer," I tease.

He shakes his head. "You're perfect."

I duck my head, because it feels like too much. I'm having a hard time believing that any of this is real. It feels too good. "I'm waiting for the shoe to drop," I say. "For this all to be one big ten-year-long joke."

"It's not."

"I know. I just—" I stop, trying to think of what I mean. "Things like this don't happen."

We spin slowly in a circle, and it's effortless following his lead. "Consider this the dance we should have had that night."

"I think for that I'd need a tiara."

He chuckles, and I feel the vibration through his body. "This is the Plaza, I can see what strings I can pull. If they were willing to set up a basketball hoop, I'm sure there's a tiara around here somewhere."

"That's okay," I say. "If it's all right with you, I'd rather have this dance be who we are now, not who we were."

"That's fine with me," he says softly.

With these heels on I can just see over his shoulder, and Lorraine is behind him now, watching us and grinning like an idiot. I bite down on my lip to suppress my enormous smile.

We dance in silence, and it feels so good, so comfortable. His thumb is stroking softly on my back and his lips rest gently against my temple. I close my eyes and let him guide us, reveling in the moment. I know that I said I didn't want this to be a dance to make up for prom, but it still feels significant, like there's a measure of healing in this for both of us.

The song comes to an end, and for a moment the ballroom is quiet. There's a spell cast over it, everyone caught in the nostalgia of the moment. And then another upbeat song comes on and it's broken, and people start to dance again. "Drink?" he asks, already helping me through the crowd toward the bar.

He's right, I'm thirsty.. There's a bunch of people near the bar, including some of the guys that swarmed us earlier. Adam spots a table and asks, "What would you like? I'll grab it."

"Vodka cranberry." I need something stronger than wine.

He nods. "I'll be right back."

As soon as he's gone, I feel hands on my shoulders. "Oh. My. God. OLLIE." It's Lor.

"I admit," I say, "you were right and I'm forever indebted to you, et cetera."

"Girl, you don't owe me a thing."

I smile. "All the same, I think I'm going to by you some chocolate."

"The good kind please."

"As if I would ever get anything less than the best for you." I fake a gasp. And then I glance toward the bar. Adam is still waiting for the drinks, so I've got a couple minutes. "I need help."

Lor makes a face, "From what I saw you don't need any help at all."

"I think I—" I swallow. "I think I want to invite him home."

"So do it. You deserve it."

I sigh. "Yeah, but remember the last time I asked a guy home? That ended pretty badly."

"You can't possibly be comparing Adam Carlisle to douchey Tinder guy."

"Well—"

Lorraine leans forward and grabs me by the shoulders. "This isn't the same. You guys have known each other for years. He's the one that approached you, I saw it. And the way you two were dancing?" She fans her face. "There's no chance that he says no."

"But if he does, I'm going to be an absolute mess."

"If he does," she says, "I'm going to punch him in the nuts."

I start to giggle, because it's so ridiculous and I have no doubt whatsoever that she would follow through. I see Adam step up to the bar. "Okay, he's going to come back now."

"You can do this, just breathe, and good luck."

"Okay." The thought of doing this kind of makes me want to throw up from anxiety, but her confidence helps. "Before you go, Joey Lancaster?"

She shrugs, "He was good in high school, and he's hotter now. I'm thinking I'll see if he's learned any new moves."

I laugh and roll my eyes. "Go get 'em tiger."

Adam turns and makes his way back to me, and nerves punch me in the gut. I clench my hands into fists and release them to try to relieve some of the shaking.

"Here you go." Adam passes me my

drink, and he has one of his own.

I take a big sip, and it helps a little. "I have something to ask you, and I'm nervous."

"Okay, I promise I'm not that scary."

"It's just that the last time I did this it didn't go well."

Adam looks confused. "Okay."

"I was wondering if you wanted to come back to my apartment." My stomach rolls with nerves and maybe the alcohol was a bad idea because now I feel kind of light-headed. I can't remember when I ate last. My palms are sweaty and I'm hanging on Adam's expression figuring out if I'm going to need to go bury myself in a hole in Central Park.

His face turns from confusion to a perfect, beautiful smile. He throws back his drink in one go, and puts it down on the table. "Ready to go when you are."

Sweet, pure, relief floods my system, and I copy him by finishing my drink in one long sip. "Okay, I'm ready."

CHAPTER NINE

Adam

I take Olivia by the hand and walk through the ballroom as quickly as I can without drawing attention or making Ollie think that the only reason I said yes was for sex. I mean, I fucking hope there's sex because my dick has been as hard as a rock since I kissed her, and every time I look at her in that dress, I think I lose a little more blood flow to my brain.

But it's more than that. I want to be with her, in her space, in her bed. I want to talk to her and find out all the things I didn't when I first had the chance. I want to find out what kind of things she likes to read and do, and then I want to do all those things with her. I want to know how her family is and what her life has been like these last ten years. I didn't lie to her when I said that I'd thought about her. I have thought about her a lot in the last ten years, but I never thought that this would happen.

If I were in her position, I honestly don't know if I would have forgiven me. I should have done so much more to help her. Telling her what really happened would have been a good fucking start.

I really should have asked her if I could kiss her first, but I didn't see another way to show her my real reaction. And god, kissing Ollie is like…

I don't have words for it. Never in my

life have I had a kiss like that. Who knows if it's ten years of pent-up emotions or the fact that she looks stunning tonight, but I'd be stupid if I gave up this opportunity, sex or no.

She was so nervous asking me to come over, it makes me wonder why. It's something I want to ask, but this isn't the time or place to ask it. I let go of her for a second so I can pull out a tip for the doorman, and he flags down a cab for us. I hold the door open for her and she slides in first. As soon as I'm inside, I pull her close. I don't want her to think that there's any hesitation on my part. At all. I don't know if I can express how much I actually want this, and this is an easy way to help with that.

Besides, it's not exactly a hardship to have Ollie this close to me. I can feel the shape of her so clearly through her dress, and yet it still feels like there's so much hidden.

She gives her address to the driver and off we go, speeding towards the 59th Street Bridge. She looks at me, and her expression is puzzled in the passing streetlights. "This is so weird."

"What?"

"You're here with me. We're going to my apartment."

I lean down close so that the cab driver doesn't hear me. "Want to be a cliché and make out in the cab?"

"I'm pretty much always down for being a cliché," she says.

I kiss her, and the way her lips open under mine has my cock harder than it's ever been and need tugging in my gut to have more of her. I pull her toward me until she's practically in my lap and I can stroke my hand down across her hip, savor her curves. She tastes like the cranberry in the drink that she just had, and I can smell whatever perfume she has on, light lavender and vanilla and I love it.

When I decided to go to the reunion, I thought I would be there for an hour and then go home; never to see anyone again. This is way, way better. The way she's leaning into me, kissing me back, I wish we'd had this when we were eighteen. But then again, maybe it's better that we're trying this now. Later. After having time to let the rest of that go.

It seems like only minutes before the

cab pulls to a stop in front of an apartment building in Queens. One of the older ones, easily pre-war. We disentangle long enough for me to pay the cab driver and then I help her out of the cab. The lobby of her building has been updated, a nice glass door and crystal chandelier decorate the marble foyer. There's a code lock on the door too.

She lets us in the first door to the foyer, and the second door to the stairs. "It's a walk-up," she says. "Sorry."

I saw the building from outside—it's only a three-story building, and that's how many floors we go up. Stopping in front of a door that has panes of frosted glass, she turns to me. "Would you mind waiting outside for a couple of minutes?"

"Why? You have someone else inside?"

128

I tease.

She blushes, and it's the perfect shade of pink. I want to see if I can make her blush other places, in other ways. "No, it's just I wasn't exactly expecting company. I want to clean a couple of things up."

I laugh. "I don't care about that."

"You say that now, but you might."

"I won't. You haven't seen a mess until you've seen the residents' locker room."

Ollie bites her lip, and it's adorable. "Still, I could just pick a couple of things up."

"What if I promise to keep my eyes closed until you're happy."

"Promise?"

I won't lie, I'm curious to see what

exactly she thinks is messy. "I promise I'll give you at least a minute."

"That's all I need." She gets a key from under the mat and unlocks the door. "My key is still with my stuff at Bergdorf's. Lorraine is having it messengered over tomorrow. Now close your eyes."

I do, and she takes my hand and leads me inside. In my head I start counting to sixty, and I hear the sounds of Ollie kicking off her shoes, hurried footsteps and the clink of some glasses. Her footsteps disappear deeper into the apartment and I hear shuffling and a few more sounds like dishware clinking. "Can I open my eyes?" I ask, even though I've only counted to forty-five.

"Not yet! Just one more minute."

There's a few thumps, and her footsteps running quickly past me. More clinking. "Okay, I guess that's as good as I can do."

I open my eyes, and look around. Her apartment is nice, dove gray walls and a simple foyer with a door to the left into the kitchen. I see some dishes in the sink and some towels in a pile, but nothing else that I would immediately assign as dirty or messy.

Ollie's dress is now pooling around her feet, and I can see her bare toes peeking out from beneath the dress. She's fidgeting like she's waiting for me to pass judgment on her and the apartment. "I like your place," I say.

"But—"

"I'm not sure what you call messy, but

this isn't it."

She bites her lip again. "Okay."

We go into the living room and I see a few things here and there out of place, a little clutter. But it makes the place look lived in, not messy. "Do you want something to drink?"

"Sure."

"Okay," she says, heading back to the kitchen. Her face looks relieved that she has something to do, and I realize that she's nervous. I suppose with our history that it makes sense.

While she's in the kitchen, I take the time to look around the room. There's a couch that looks really comfortable, a small TV, a wall filled with an asymmetrical collage of art prints and a couple of large bookshelves. So she's a reader more than a television person. Given what I know of Ollie from high school, it fits.

The shelves are more eclectic than I would have thought, though. Just scanning I see business books, biographies, fiction, mythology and poetry. So she reads everything. Good to know. Out of the corner of my eye, I see the *World's Waterfall* series on the top shelf. The third book looks particularly beat up, and I wonder if it's the same copy that she used to own. I'll have to ask her sometime.

"Here you go," she says, and I turn to take one of the glasses of wine that she's holding.

"Thank you." I nod to the bookshelves.

"So you still like to read."

She sighs, but in a relaxed way. This is safe territory for her. "Yeah. Always have. I try to make time for it still, even though I'd like to do more."

"I wish I read more, but a lot of days I barely have the energy to fall into bed."

Ollie sits down on the couch and tucks her feet up under her. "Are things that hard at the hospital?"

"No, not always." I sit on the other end of the couch. "But it's Columbia. We've got a lot of difficult cases. And in pediatrics, kids can be hard. They don't always get what's happening, and it can be rough."

She takes a sip of her wine. "I'm sorry."

"I'm not," I say. "I like what I do. But it helps to acknowledge the difficulties."

"Yeah," Ollie says. She seems way more comfortable now, and I wonder if it's because we're not talking about her. "Do you have something you want to do inside pediatrics? A specialty within a specialty?"

I shake my head. "No. General pediatrics. But things can get complicated with kids, so even though I'm considered 'general' it still feels like a specialty. You get pulled into all kinds of strange cases just because things can go wrong really fast in little humans."

The wine she's chosen is good, and I know that I'm a bit drunk with this and the drinks I had at the reunion. But not so drunk that I'm about to get sloppy. She takes another sip, and I like the way she's relaxing. Like this is a normal and she's not about to bolt.

"So you went to college, where?"

"Dartmouth," she says.

I grin. I knew it would be somewhere amazing. "That's awesome. And then what happened?"

"You want my whole life story?" she asks, cheeks turning pink again.

"I do," I say. "I want to know everything."

"Everything is a lot."

I nod. "True. How about just for now, you tell me about your job."

"My job is boring." She says it so

automatically that it doesn't even sound like her saying it.

I move a little closer on the couch. "Do you say it's boring because you actually think it's boring? Or because you assume other people already think that it's boring?"

Ollie blinks, and looks at me suddenly. "No one's ever asked that before."

"Well what's the truth?"

She thinks for a second. "It's like half and half. There are a lot of parts of my job that are boring. Repetitive. But that's not always a bad thing. It can be comforting. There's no room for error when you're dealing with numbers. You always know where you stand." A pause. "But I really hate learning the updated tax code every year."

I laugh. "Yeah, I doubt anyone would like that kind of reading."

"You'd be surprised," she says. "There are people who are even nerdier than me."

"Nothing wrong with being nerdy," I say, moving closer again. We're close to touching now.

She laughs into her wine glass. "You're the least nerdy person that I can think of."

"Trust me, everyone is a nerd about something. Besides, we haven't seen each other in ten years. I could be the world's biggest super-nerd and you wouldn't know."

"That's true," she says, leaning closer to me. "But you don't look like a nerd."

"Something that works in my favor," I say softly, closing the distance between us. I take the glass out of her hand and put them both on the table. Then, reaching out, I slip my hand behind her neck. "Is this all right?" I ask.

"Yes."

And then I kiss her.

CHAPTER TEN

Ollie

The wine and the vodka are making me feel warm and fuzzy. I feel comfortable now, and not as anxious. Adam leans in and kisses me, and this one is soft and slow and easy. It feels *good*.

I'm so happy that I had the guts to ask him to come here and that he said yes. I like that he tastes like wine and whiskey, and the way his fingers tease the skin around my neck. Here, when we're alone, I get to feel everything I wanted to feel while we were dancing. I don't have to worry about making a fool of myself in front of people who still hate me.

Suddenly my body is raring to go, all the arousal I shoved aside comes surging back. I pull Adam to me, and he is right there, not missing a step. He licks across my lips and it sends fire down my spine. I have to gasp for air but I don't want to stop kissing him. I want him on me, in me. It's been a long time, but even if it hadn't, the way this feels would be exquisite. There's raw chemistry between us waiting to explode, and I realize that I'm wet. That's how badly I want him.

We're lying together on the couch now, legs tangled together, and my dress is up almost to my hips. One of my straps is falling off my shoulder, lowering my neckline to a dangerous level. And the fact it has no back... it feels like I'm showing more skin than I'm covering. I feel sexy and powerful, and I pull back far enough to see Adam's face. He knows the state of my dress too, I can see it in his eyes. The want and need that makes mine that much more powerful.

"Ollie, I need to ask," he says, chest rising and falling heavily. "How far is this going tonight?"

There's cold drip of fear in my gut. "Do you want to stop?"

"God, no." He lets his lips fall to my collarbone, tasting my skin. "But I don't want to go faster than you're ready for."

I arch my body into his, enjoying the sound he makes in his throat. "I'm ready," I say. "I think we've both been ready for this for a long time." I take the time to trace his face with my fingers. There's a barely there scratch of stubble on his jaw, and the line of it makes me understand why people say some jaws can cut glass. His nose has a little bump on the top, and I wonder if he broke it. And then his eyes, a perfect green that's staring down into me, and I think I could get lost there for a long time.

"Then I don't want to stay on the couch."

"Is it uncomfortable?" I ask. "Sometimes I think this couch can be lumpy, and it's older."

He chuckles against my skin. "Ollie."

"Yeah."

"I don't want to stay on the couch like someone you bring home to fool around with.

This is different than that to me."

What he's saying sinks in. "Oh. Okay."

Adam's lips press to the skin just below my ear. "Let me take you to bed."

I shiver, goosebumps rising on my skin from his kiss and his words. And then I nod.

"Which one is your bedroom?"

"Here," I sit up, about to show him around, when he beats me to it. He's up on his feet and he scoops me up off the couch like I'm weightless. "Which door?" he asks, smiling.

"French doors."

Pushing the door open with his foot, Adam carries me into my bedroom, and I'm so grateful that I'm actually in the habit of making my bed. He claims he doesn't care about the mess, but I'm still skeptical.

He lays me down on the bed, and then he's over me again. "I'm going to go slow, because I don't want either of us to forget this."

I'm going to say something, but his lips are on my shoulder and I forget all the words. He's tracing the lines of me with his mouth, moving to my neck and down the center of my chest, slow and deliberate. Each kiss raises more goosebumps on my skin, sends more arousal spiraling down into my core where it stays and builds.

Gently he helps me out of the straps of my dress and peels it back. I'm not wearing a bra, and my nipples are already hard from his attention. There's a short intake of breath, and he stares at me. I realize this is the

145

moment where there's no turning back. The look on his face, awe and wonder and lust makes me pull him down to me again.

"I want to see you," I say, trying to unbutton his shirt, but Adam catches my hands by the wrists.

"You will, I promise. But first, I want to savor you." The dark roughness of his voice slithers down my spine and I feel myself dampen further.

Savor. Like I'm a flavor that he wants more of. Like he's going to taste me. *God, yes.*

My dress is down to my hips, and his mouth is on my skin again. He moves slowly, drawing a line of pleasure and fire down between my breasts. One hand reaches out to squeeze, and my back arches off the bed. He laughs.

"What?" I feel the blood rushing to my face before I can even form the words to speak the question, and Adam smiles. "I love the way you blush," he says, "especially when you do it here." He draws his finger down the path that his mouth followed. "But I still want to know why you're blushing."

I know why, but I don't want to say. I don't want to scare him away.

Adam's hands cradle my face. "What are you afraid of?"

"So much," I whisper. "And I don't want to ruin this."

He pulls back so he's kneeling on the bed and pulls me with him, so that we're upright together. It feels less vulnerable, even if I'm still half naked, still aching for him to touch me.

"Tonight, let that go," he says. "I want you, and I'm not going to leave unless you ask me to."

I don't know how he knew that's what I needed, but I kiss him, wrap my arms around his neck, and the scratch of his shirt on my breasts makes me gasp into his mouth.

"Why were you blushing?"

"They're sensitive," I say, voice breathy. "And it's—I like it when—" I can't seem to get the words out, but that's all he needs.

Adam's hands come up and then he's touching me, thumbs rolling across my nipples and I feel that everywhere. I have to close my eyes, because it feels so damn good.

"Oh," he says, running his thumb over me again, watching me shake. "I see. You were embarrassed to tell me that you like this?"

He does it again with both hands and I moan. If he keeps doing that I think I might come. It's happened before and I know it's not common but god every time someone touches my nipples I'm in heaven. "Yes," I say. I don't know if it's the answer to his question or a request for more. Either. Both.

I'm on my back again now, and suddenly his mouth is there, covering my nipple while he toys with the other one. Adam's tongue swirls around my skin and I can't breathe. He sucks, pulling my skin taut and then grazing his teeth across me and oh god I'm so wet that I think I might be ruining the dress and I can't even worry about it because holy fuck.

He pinches my left nipple between his fingers, twisting and pulling just hard enough to shoot a burst of fiery heat down to my clit. My breath is coming in gasps, and I can't believe that he's doing this. I've never had someone spend this much time on my breasts, just enjoying them. The last time I came like this was an accident, and the guy was so freaked out that he had to stop.

Adam switches his attention from one nipple to the other and fuck—

The roughness of his tongue on me is bringing me higher. Higher. He squeezes me, and oh god. I gasp, my body going rigid as pleasure splinters through me from deep inside. It moves outward, and I'm lost in the sensation. It's brilliant, like a flare—just a flash and then gone, but it's beautiful, and I'm still trying to catch my breath.

I open my eyes to Adam looking down at me, searching my face. "You should never, ever, be embarrassed about that," he says.

"Other men have said differently."

"Then those men are idiots. That's one of the hottest things I've ever seen." He presses a kiss to my lips, "and if you come that hard when I play with your tits, I can't wait to see what happens when I reach your pussy."

"Oh—" I'm cut off because he's back at my breasts again, taking each nipple into his mouth and giving each one a long, deep suck that pulls on my clit and makes me shiver. He could stop right now and I'd be satisfied. But then again, I'm curious about what's going to happen next. I've never had anyone affect me this way, and I think it's going to be amazing.

Adam's tongue licks down my stomach, teasing me, tracing lines on my hipbones and across, just above where my dress has pooled. I'm soaking with anticipation, and grab the blanket on the bed to hold myself back from grabbing him and trying to make him go faster.

He hooks his fingers in the dress and pulls it down my hips. I close my eyes listening to the slithering sound as the silk hits the floor. I'm naked with Adam Carlisle. This is a dream, and I don't want to open my eyes and risk waking up.

His mouth gets closer and closer: the top of my thigh, the edge of my hip, the smooth skin of my mound where my legs are pressed together.

Another kiss there, insistent, and Adam's hands are on my hips pulling me closer to his mouth. Then his tongue darts out, and I gasp and I relax, letting my legs open.

Another dart of his tongue meets my clit and holy fuck that feels so good. "Mmm," Adam makes a sound low in his throat, and god it's the hottest thing. He's turned on by me, wants to *savor* me. I want him to lick me again, I want to feel what he can do with his mouth because if he can kiss me like that then —

My whole body tightens when he touches me, a kiss on my inner thigh and then closer. Just a flick of tongue on my skin. I don't know where he's going to touch me next, and it might drive me crazy. I open my eyes and the sight of Adam's head buried between my legs sends another burst of wetness gushing from me, and Adam laughs.

"I love how wet you are."

And then he seals his mouth over my clit and sucks. The world turns white, and I come instantly. I'm too turned on for anything else to happen. My whole body jerks against his mouth but he keeps me still with his hands, tongue swirling around my clit as he sucks me deep. Pleasure fizzes through my limbs, lighting that I have to contain, and I moan out loud.

He doesn't stop, instead, he licks me in long, slow strokes that make me jump and send sparks swirling through my body. God.

"Adam," I say. I'm going to tell him that it's enough, that I can't take anymore and that he can stop, but then his tongue slips inside my pussy and I go blind with pleasure. The words I was forming blur into nothing. "Fuuuuck." Just one drawn-out word that make him chuckle. The vibrations are good. So good.

He's fucking me with his tongue now, licking deep, trying to reach the G-spot, and oh my god he's almost there. So close. But not quite. He moves his hand so that his thumb is lazily circling my clit and my muscles start to shake. I'm on the edge of another orgasm, but not quite there. Not quite. I'm instead caught in that place of pleasure that's deep and just on the edge. I'm drowning in it, pulsing close to the edge and being pulled back again and

155

again.

Adam sucks at my entrance before pulling back. His voice is rough, and I feel it on my skin. "I like the way you taste."

Covering my clit with his mouth again, I want to say something, but nothing comes out but another moan. This one louder. I can't even think about how I'm embarrassing myself because it feels so damn good.

He slips a finger inside me, and then two, and then three. I'm so wet that he slips in without a problem and suddenly I'm so, so full. He curves his fingers, and *shit* there it is. He strokes across my G-spot and I cry out because it's there, I'm close to falling off a cliff and into an ocean of pleasure that I'm not sure I'll resurface from.

One more stroke, and I fall. I might be gasping, might be screaming, I'm not sure. The orgasm is pure light, it sears through my body and crackles through my nerves and I'm shaking and god yes this is exactly what I want.

Adam is still there, stroking me with his tongue and his fingers and it feels like the pleasure just keeps going. I can't see or breathe or hear, it's just pleasure. He slows down, but my body still has spasms, little mini-orgasms. I didn't know I could come this much. I don't remember a time where I've done it this hard or this close together.

I'm panting on the bed, and I look down to see Adam smiling at me. "Holy shit," I say. "You are very good at that."

"I'm glad you think so."

157

He shrugs out of his tuxedo jacket and I can't believe he's still in his suit after all this. "I should have made you take your jacket off."

"It's off now."

And other things are coming off too. He takes of his shirt one button at a time and I get to see that perfect chest and stomach appear. It doesn't disappoint. He's lean, and I'm amazed that he has a body like this while he's a resident. But I'm glad that he does. I follow the lines of him from his chest across a set of perfect abs and lower to the waist of his pants where he has those lines that dip beneath and I want to lick them.

He drops his shirt to the floor and kicks off his shoes. "I feel like there should be some music," he says, teasing. "Since I'm stripping for you."

"Next time," I say, "because I want you naked now."

"Yes, Ma'am."

His pants fall to the floor, and through his boxer briefs I can already see how hard he is, and how big. His cock is straining against the fabric, and I want it. He's about to take them off, but I stop him, moving to the edge of the bed and pulling him closer by the hips. "Wait."

God, he's big. I run my fingers across him through the fabric and I see all his muscles tighten. I stroke him again, and look up to see the way his eyes are focused on me, so dark, so filled with want.

I hook my fingers on the sides of his underwear and pull them down, letting his cock spring free. It stands proudly straight out from his body, and I have to reach out and touch it. He's so hard, and when my fingers stroke his skin he closes his eyes.

He savored me, and now I want to savor him. I lean forward, but he stops me an inch before my lips touch him. "I want that," he says. *"Believe me,* I want that. But if you touch me with those lips I'm going to come, and I want to be inside you when I do."

I smirk at him, suddenly very much liking the idea that I've turned him on so much that he doesn't think he'll last. I lean back on the bed and arch my back, showing off my breasts. "How do you want me?"

CHAPTER ELEVEN

Adam

I don't think the words she's saying register for a second. The sight of her draped across the bed, confident as queen has me frozen in place. I can't respond.

Then she asks again, "Tell me what you want."

What I want is to be inside her as quickly as possible. I fumble for my wallet in my pants on the floor and grab a condom from my wallet and roll it on. "I want you," I say, joining her on the bed.

I love the feel of her underneath me, finally skin on skin. I kiss her until she closes her eyes, and stroke down her side. I don't think I'll get enough of just *touching* her. She's soft and firm and so fucking gorgeous I can't keep my head on straight. I've been on the edge of coming this whole time, and I don't know how long I can last. I know that I would have lost is the second I felt her tongue on my cock.

Jesus, just thinking about her tongue on my cock...

I reach between us, fitting myself against her entrance, and I watch her eyes fly open to meet mine while I push in slowly. She moans, and it's the sexist fucking sound. Her pussy is tight, squeezing me as I push in and in and I think I'm in heaven. I could stay here and be happy.

The fact that she's so tight even though

she's come three times, shit. I'm all the way in, and it's a tight fit. She squeezes down on me and I think that I might black out. "You feel so fucking good."

I try to stay still, because I'm big and I don't want to hurt her, but all I want to do is to fuck her until she's screaming and senseless.

Ollie pulls my face to hers and kisses me. I hope she can taste herself on my tongue and know how much I enjoyed it. I start to move, because I can't hold myself back anymore. I pull back and sink in, and it's sweet delicious friction. Shit.

I have to hold my breath and tense all my muscles, but I keep the rhythm steady. Speed up a little and stay there. Not too fast.

"Adam," Ollie says, and I look down at her. Her eyes are glazed with pleasure, and I love that look. "Take me."

My heart stops in my chest. "What?"

One of her hands grips my side, and I can feel her nails there urging me on. The other pulls my face down to hers. "Take me. You're holding back."

I don't need her to say it again. I reach down, tilting her hips up into mine, and pull back. I drive into her in one stroke, and I don't stop. Fuck. I plunge into her again and again and again and it feels so good and in a part of my mind I can't believe that this is Ollie, that I'm finally fulfilling every fantasy I've had for the last ten years. I want to take her hard and fast and I want to make it last as long as humanly possible.

She's grabbing the sheets, holding on while I fuck her, and her tits are bouncing with every thrust. God, I want to fuck them. I want to fuck them and make her come from just fucking her tits.

I'm close to coming, and I want to be even closer to her. Pulling out, I grab her hips and turn her over. She's right there with me, and I slip back in, folding myself over her, so that every part of us is touching. God, her ass pressed up into my hips feels so good, and the way she's taking me without missing a beat— I'm going to come.

But not without her.

I reach between us, and search for her clit with my fingers. She's so wet and my fingers slip and slide around it, but I hear her gasping, and I feel the tension in her body. I close my eyes, thrusting harder, faster, circling with my fingers until I she's begging. "Yes, yes, yes, yes." It's a chant or a prayer and it matches the rhythm of my fucking.

"Adam!" Ollie screams my name, and I feel the gush of wetness on my hand as she comes, and I can't hold back. I thrust deep, reaching a speed I didn't think I could, and there—

My vision disappears and lightning flashes up my spine and outward. Bursts of heat and pleasure ripple through my body, and I call Ollie's name.

I empty myself into the condom, every pull of my orgasm is deep and sharp and it takes every last bit of me.

I come back to myself, panting, holding

Ollie against me, still buried inside her. My lips are at her neck, and I can see the faint sheen of sweat on her skin. I don't pull out of her, not yet. I just lower us to the bed, keeping her close. Her pussy squeezes down on me, an after-effect of her own orgasm, and I groan.

I've never come like that. Ever.

What the hell just happened?

"Adam," she says, and her voice is raw from her screams and moans. She doesn't say anything else. But I know. I wrap my arm around her, and I like that I can touch so much of her at once. Our legs are tangled, my chest pressed against her back, my arm spreading across her hip and breasts to her shoulder. I kiss her neck, breathing in the lingering scent of her perfume with the new smell of sex, and I can feel myself twitch.

Like my cock is thinking it might want another go. I slowly slip out of her, and I feel the loss. I want to be back inside that soft heat. It's perfect.

"Where's your bathroom?" I ask softly.

"The door before the kitchen."

I quickly make my way there and get rid of the condom and clean myself off before going back to the bedroom. While I was gone, Ollie got under the covers, and I slip under them with her. We're face to face now, but I still want her closer. I put an arm behind her so that we're touching all the way down our bodies, breathing each other's air.

"Hi," she says, a cute smile on her face.

"Hi."

"That was...that was very good. Thank

you."

I chuckle. "You're welcome, but I think I'm the one that needs to say it. It was..."

"Yeah me too." She sighs, "I owe Lorraine a very big present."

"Maybe I'll send her flowers," I say.

"She'd really like that," Ollie says sleepily, snuggling down into me. It makes my cock jump and stiffen and she laughs.

"What are you doing tomorrow?"

"Nothing." She yawns. "Just a normal boring Sunday for me."

"Good." I lay back and take her with me so she's draped across my chest. "I want to take you out where there aren't a hundred of our former classmates there to watch us."

Her head pops up. "You're staying?"

"If you'll let me."

She tries to hide her smile by ducking her head, but I still see it. "Yes."

I stroke my hand down her back and I feel her relax. She doesn't realize that the only thing that would make me leave right now is her throwing me out on my ass.

The high of everything is beginning to wear off, and I feel sleep coming, and I can feel Ollie's breathing going steady too. "Good night, Olivia."

"Night."

CHAPTER TWELVE

Ollie

I wake up slowly. First with just the awareness that I'm awake, and then realizing that there is someone else in my bed with me. And finally feeling the arm draped across me and the body behind me.

Suddenly I'm *wide awake*. Oh my god, Adam Carlisle is in my bed. I had sex with Adam last night, and not only that but it was the best sex of my life. I open my eyes, and my bedroom is dim. I can see that the sun is already well up from the light behind the shades, but I don't care. It's Sunday, and I get to spend it with Adam.

I try not to move, or at least move slowly, because I don't want to wake him up. But as I'm moving slowly I realize something: he's hard. I suppose that I could wake him up on purpose, my way.

He doesn't stir when I slip out from under his hand, and duck under the covers, and he doesn't stir when I find his cock with my hand, stroking it gently. I press my lips to the tip of him, tasting the salt there. I feel him move then, and I lick him like I would a lollipop.

"Ollie?" Adam's voice is bleary and confused.

I take him into my mouth then, sucking on the head of him and he swears, throwing back the blankets. He stares at me in shock, and I take him deeper causing him to close his eyes.

"Good morning," I say, pulling back and licking down his shaft until I reach the base of him.

I cover every inch of him with my tongue, and I watch his breath start to come faster. Finally, I make it back to the tip, and he groans when I sink down onto him again. Adam reaches out, tangling his fingers in my hair and holding on, guiding me with angle and thrust. He moves me faster, deeper, gripping my hair with both hands now.

Yes. I close my eyes and let him lead. He groans when I take him to the back of my mouth, the tip of him slipping into my throat. I pull back for a second, gasping for air. But only for a second, because I dive down onto him again, and I want him to come as hard as he made me come last night.

He works me on his cock in smooth strokes, up and down, and I like the feel of him between his lips. I suck hard on him, using my tongue whenever I can. But I let him lead, his entire body taut as he fucks my mouth.

"Ollie," Adam says, a second before he plunges deeper than he's gone before. His cock jerks, and I'm flooded with his salty cum and I swallow as quickly as I can. He's filling my mouth, and I do my best to catch it all. He's still thrusting in, one long moan coming from his mouth, and then he lets me go, spent.

I finish swallowing, licking his cock clean while he watches. The way he's looking at me right now, like I'm something to eat, is something I'll never forget.

"Holy shit, Ollie," he says, still catching his breath. "Good morning."

"I'm hungry," I say. "Want some breakfast?"

"Sure."

I hop out of the bed, practically running out of the room because I just had Adam's cock in my mouth and I both love that and am somehow embarrassed by it. Eggs. I can make eggs. I put the frying pan on the stove and crack some eggs into it, and dig around in my fridge for some sprinkled cheese. I throw some of that in the pan, too.

Adam appears in the doorway to the kitchen, still completely naked, and I'm distracted by the sight of his body in the daylight. God, he's gorgeous.

"If you're going to cook naked on a regular basis, I may have to stay over more often."

I blush. "I'd be okay with that."

"But right now," he says, crossing the kitchen to me and pressing me against the wall, "you ran away from bed before I had the chance to properly say good morning."

"You said you were hungry."

"I am, but I was about to say that it could wait."

He's so close it's overwhelming, and the fact that he's touching me, running his hands down my arms and his chest pressed against mine has me panting with need. "Wait for what?"

A hand slides down my stomach, farther, until his fingers reach my pussy and he slips one inside. "For me to see how wet you are and decide what I'm going to do about it."

The sound that comes from me can only be described as a whimper.

"What should I do about it?" he asks, but he's not asking me, just musing out loud. "I could use my fingers on you until you're shaking and my hand is covered in you. I could put you up on this countertop and fuck you until you scream my name again. I could take you against this wall right now." His fingers are still moving inside me, and I close my eyes, waiting to see what he'll do. "It's a pity I didn't come prepared," he said.

"Prepared?"

He adds a second finger and I gasp. "I didn't bring any more condoms. Don't worry, I won't make that mistake again." A third finger, and at this angle it's a stretch. "I plan on taking you against a wall very soon, Ollie. And on this countertop. And in your shower. And in my shower. Every place you can think of, I'm going to fuck you."

"Yes," I breathe. Adam's fingers are moving in and out of me steadily, stroking across my G-spot and deeper. He knows just what he's doing to make me shudder in pleasure. His thumb brushes my clit and I moan into his shoulder. I'm on my tip-toes and holding him is the only thing that's keeping me on my feet. My legs are shaking and weak but I don't want him to stop, please don't stop please—

I look at Adam, and he looks at me, and he doesn't hesitate as he slips the last finger inside me. My eyes flutter closed again and oh god the only thing I can do is feel right now. I'm stuffed full, fuller than with his cock, and he's stretching me, fucking me with his hand and teasing my clit and I think my heart's going to explode it's pounding so hard.

I'm straining, trying to hold myself back from the edge because I want to make it last. Adam's other hand reaches into my hair, pulling my head back so he can see my face. "Let go, Ollie."

I shake my head, it feels too good. I need to hold on. It can't get any better than this.

He presses down on my clit with his thumb, hard. "Come."

I do, pleasure bursting outward like a whirlwind through my body. I was wrong, this is so much better. "Oh god, yes!" I keep saying it, and he keeps me fucking me, and the orgasm never seems to end. It's dripping down my legs and onto his fingers and I'm shaking and the pleasure is sweet and sharp and it crashes over me in a final wave before disappearing and leaving me gasping.

I lean back against the wall, panting, and watch as Adam lifts his fingers to his hand, licking them clean. "Morning," he says with a grin.

I grin back at him. Because this is strange and weird and amazing and I didn't think that I could be this happy. And I never thought I would be this happy because of Adam.

180

Suddenly the burning smell reaches my nose. "Shit." I spring around Adam and shut off the burner under the eggs, but they're already smoking. I grab a dishtowel and wave it frantically at the smoke detector. Thankfully it doesn't go off. My smoke detector is a real bitch and once it starts going off it really doesn't like to stop.

"Well, I guess that's that for that breakfast." I glance at Adam and smile, "Definitely worth it though."

"Good." he pulls me in for a kiss. "Whatever will we do now?"

"The bodega down the street has really good food. I'll run out and get us some coffee and donuts and maybe something not entirely sugar."

"Works for me," he says.

"Good." I run to my room and throw on some yoga pants and a sweatshirt and throw my hair into a bun so it looks less like I had wild sex all night.

Adam is by the door as I leave. "Now that I know what's under there I won't be able to get it out of my head."

"I could say the same," I say, glancing down at his cock, which is hardening in front of me, "but I don't have to imagine right now."

He chuckles. "Hurry back so I can ruin the second breakfast too."

"I will," I say, grabbing my key.

There's a box outside the foyer door, and I see that it's my clothes and wallet from

Bergdorf's. Perfect. The bodega knows me and would have gladly added the food to my tab, but now I don't have to do that. I leave my clothes in the box and head down to the end of the block to Marsha's. It's really the hub of our little neighborhood, and everyone knows everyone.

I order a couple of coffees and doughnuts and one of their giant sausage egg and cheese bagel sandwiches. They're so large that I never manage to finish them on my own, so I figure we can split it, or Adam can eat the whole thing.

It doesn't take long for them to make up my order, just a few minutes, so I text Lorraine.

How did things go with Joey?

An almost immediate response.

He's a good time, but not exactly mind blowing. But who knows, maybe I can whip him into shape. :)

And immediately:

But don't try to hide from me, you and Adam are the real story here! How did THAT go?

I laugh to myself. She's nosy, but I love her.

I'm at Marsha's right now getting breakfast for us.

HE'S STILL THERE OLLIE? OH MY GOD!!!

I'll tell you about it later.

Yes, you will. You will tell me every little gory detail until I'm begging you to stop.

Fat chance of that, but I'm not going to argue that point yet.

Lol. I'll call you in a bit. Not sure what the plan for today is.

They call my name, and I grab the bag with my food and the little cardboard tray that has the drinks and head back to my apartment. I manage to grab the box from the foyer with my clothes in it too.

"Okay," I say, walking into the apartment. "I didn't know what kind of doughnuts you like, so I got a bunch, plus they have a breakfast sandwich that's truly an impressive size, if you feel like that."

No response.

"Adam?"

I set the food on the countertop in the kitchen, and walk through my apartment. He's not in the bathroom, and by the time I reach the bedroom I have a pit in the bottom of my stomach. His clothes are gone from where they were lying on my floor. Well, shit. How did I not see that coming?

When I get back to the kitchen, I see a piece of paper that I missed, and I feel like a bucket of icy relief has been dumped on my head. At least he didn't take off without leaving a note. The handwriting on the note is much neater than I would expect for a doctor, which is good. I've never understood why it's not mandatory for people prescribing medication to have absolutely perfect handwriting.

Ollie,

I am so sorry. I forgot that I had lunch with

my father today. It's been scheduled for a while—not
something I'd really like to be doing—and he's not
the kind of person who takes well on being canceled
on. I didn't have your number, but I'd like to come
back tonight if that's okay? Let me know,

Adam.

There's a phone number listed there. Okay, that's good. I pull up Lorraine's contact and press call.

"Hello?"

"Hey," I say through a bite of doughnut. "Are you home yet?"

"Almost," she says, yawning. "Why?"

"Adam had to go so I have extra coffee

and doughnuts."

"I'll be there in five minutes."

True to her word, my doorbell rings barely five minutes later, and I buzz her up, mentally preparing for the onslaught of questions.

I have the cup of coffee ready to hand her when she walks through the door, and she takes it with a groan. "Oh, thank blessed Jesus. This is needed." She drops her purse on the floor and fishes a doughnut out of the bag and takes a bite, and then, "Okay, spill."

"What do you want to know?"

"Everything. But why did he have to go?"

I wince. "Well, he wasn't here when I got back with breakfast."

189

Lor almost chokes on her doughnut. "WHAT? I'm going to kill him."

"No, you're not," I say. "He left this."

I hand her the note, she reads it and then rolls her eyes. "That's such bullshit. If he didn't want to stay he could have just said so."

"If he wanted to just disappear then why did he leave his number and say that he wanted to come back?"

"Okay, fine." She makes a face. "But still, not exactly the start you're hoping for."

"I'm going to text him after you leave and see what he has to stay. But pending that, given last night, I'm willing to overlook it."

"Oh my god tell me everything."

I do...kind of. I give her the condensed version, and when I finish with what happened in the kitchen she whines. "Please, Ollie, you have to give me more details than that."

"What kind of details are you looking for?" I laugh.

"Details!" she says, biting into another doughnut. "How big is he? How many times did you orgasm? That kind of thing."

I shake my head. "Boundaries, Lor."

"Nooo. Please. I'll tell you about Joey. He has a *much* bigger dick than he did in high school, but all the same moves. But I think with practice he could be really good."

I clap my hands over my ears, "Oh my god, Lor, I don't want to know about Joey Lancaster's dick."

"You really do," she says with a pointed

smile.

Two can play that game. "Trust me, I'm good."

"God, you're such a tease."

"Bitch," I laugh, "I bought you doughnuts."

She takes another bite. "No, you bought these for your lover. These are *second hand* doughnuts. I know my true place in your heart."

"You know I'm not good at this, Lor. The whole details thing. I get all flustered, and then there's the fact that I'm not sure where this is going or how long it's going to last. I don't want to kiss and tell just yet."

Lor groans. "Ugh, I hate it when you make sense."

"I will say, it was easily the best I've ever had."

"Damn." She raises her eyebrows. "Go Adam."

We toast with our paper coffee cups. I shift gears as I remember parts of last night. "How should I get the dress back?"

"Is it still in one piece?"

I laugh. "Stop. Of course."

"Bring it by anytime, we'll see what condition it's in."

"Okay."

Lor sighs. "I've gotta go. I need a nap and a shower before I have to wait on Mrs. Diamond."

Mrs. Diamond is one of her most

particular regulars, but she can't tell me who it actually is, so we use the nickname. "Good luck with that," I say.

"I'm going to need it."

As soon as she's gone I grab Adams note and add him as a contact in my phone and type out a new message.

You know, you scared me.

I don't have to wait long for his response.

I know it looks bad. I swear that it's not what it looks like. As soon as I can make it back to your apartment, I'll be there.

Okay.

I promise. I'll even bring you a gift.

I'm intrigued.

What kind of gift?

A surprise.

I find myself biting my lip.

Surprises, in general, make me nervous.

It'll be a good surprise. I have to go, almost to the restaurant.

See you later.

Well, now that I have a better part of the afternoon alone, I need to make sure that the apartment is *actually* clean by the time he gets here. I'm not going to let him think I'm a slob. Time for music and cleaning supplies. Though cleaning my room and the kitchen are going to make me think of last night and this morning. God, I could get lost in those memories. It's going to be a long afternoon.

CHAPTER THIRTEEN

Adam

This restaurant is the last place I want to be right now. I checked my phone after Ollie went to get us breakfast and found multiple furious texts from my father about me not being at the brunch we had planned. I had completely forgotten—probably because I didn't want to go in the first place.

The last thing I wanted to do was leave Ollie like that. Not exactly a stellar start when I told her that I wanted to spend the day with her. I do, as much as I can. I just have to get this over with.

I stopped quickly at home to change so

I'm not in my tux from last night. That would bring more questions than I'm comfortable with from this particular group of people.

I walk into the restaurant and wave off the hostess. I know where I'm going. They always sit at the same table. They're already well into their meal when I walk up.

My father, my boss Dr. Pratt, and Sasha. She's the last person that I want to see. Frankly, I'm lucky that she didn't see me with Ollie last night.

I pull out my chair and sit down. "Sweetheart!" Sasha says. "You're so late, what happened?" She kisses my cheek and I stifle a cringe. I want to wipe her kiss off like I'm a kid.

Sasha is Dr. Pratt's daughter, and I

thought it would be a good idea for Sasha and me to see each other so that he would like me. I was younger then and I wanted to be successful, and Sasha agreed because dating a doctor looks good. It's the worst decision I've ever made, and a complete sham. I've never slept with Sasha. I've never kissed her. I don't want to do any of those things and never will. Over time it got complicated because Dr. Pratt *does* like me, and I didn't want that to change because I wasn't dating his daughter anymore. But now, it has to end. I'm not going to give up a chance at something real with Olivia for a fake relationship with Sasha. Sasha who almost ruined Ollie's life. If I'd known that anything would ever happen between Ollie and me, I would have broken this off years ago.

Dr. Pratt chuckles, and I realize that I haven't answered Sasha's question. "Party a little too hard with the old gang last night, Adam?"

"You could say that, yeah." I clear my throat. "Sorry to be late."

"Not a problem at all," he says. "I was just telling your father about some of your cases, but I'd love to hear about the reunion. Did you two have fun?"

I glance at Sasha, and she gives me a tiny shake of her head. She didn't tell him that we didn't go together. She clears her throat. "I wasn't there very long. I wasn't feeling well so I just said a few hellos before leaving. Adam stayed a little longer."

I manage a smile even though anger

that this is still going on is churning in my gut. "Some of the guys from the basketball team got the hotel to set up a hoop. Pretty wild stuff."

Both my dad and Dr. Pratt laugh. "Well, I'm glad you both had fun."

"Actually," I say, "There's something that we need to tell you."

Sasha quickly puts her hand on my shoulder. "Dear, I wanted to talk to you for a moment before we told them, but you were late." She looks at our fathers. "Will you excuse us for a moment?" She tosses her napkin on the table and heads towards the bar.

I nod to the dads and follow her. "Time for your daily mimosa?" I ask.

She smiles in that sickly sweet way that I've grown used to, and that I hate. "What the fuck are you doing?"

"This?" I gesture between us, "is done. I'm sick of the game and the lies. I never should have agreed to it in the first place."

"We're not done until I say we're done," she says. "I saw you last night with that slut Olivia Mitchell. This is because of her, isn't it? You were practically fucking her on the dance floor." I go cold, and Sasha pounces. "I knew it. You'd rather have the crazy suicidal freak than me?"

Anger is burning in my chest now. "Sasha, we're not even *together*. The whole relationship is fake. You really want this to go on that badly? Give me a reason why."

"Because whether you know it or not, Adam, you want me. You wouldn't have stayed this long otherwise. I know you'll come around eventually."

I shake my head because I can't believe what I'm hearing. "What?"

"I'm better than that nerd who can't even handle a little teasing. And you know it. I don't care that you're not on board yet. You will be. Besides," she says, her words cold as ice, "no one gets to reject me."

"Sasha," I sigh, "you could be happy with someone, I'm sure. But it will never be me. And there's nothing you can do to make me change my mind."

I turn and walk back to the table, and she follows me. I'm amazed that she's so calm.

I'm used to Sasha screaming and raging when she's pissed about something. The fact that she's not has me worried that there's something that I've missed. We sit back down at the table and I say, "As I was saying, there's something that we have to tell you."

"We're going to have a baby!" Sasha exclaims way too loudly, and the entire restaurant turns to look. There's stunned silence at the table and Sasha turns, throwing her arms around me in a hug. "Go along with this," she whispers, "or you'll suddenly find that you cheated on every residency exam you've ever had. And yes, there will be proof."

I can feel the blood draining from my face. Fuck.

She twists back to the table and smiles. They both look shocked, but one after another they smile. "Well," Dr. Pratt says. "This is certainly unexpected. But I can't say I'm unhappy. Congratulations, son." He holds out a hand to me and I shake it.

"Your mother is going to be thrilled," my dad says. I can tell he's not exactly happy with me for springing this on him, but he's not going to say anything now. Not in front of Dr. Pratt. "She'd be even more thrilled if there's a wedding to help plan," he says pointedly.

"We've talked about that," Sasha says, putting a hand on my arm. "We're going to wait until after Adam's residency, so he can focus on his studies first. We'll work out the details of the wedding later."

No we fucking will not. I don't know what her plan is here. How does she plan to produce a baby? Is she hoping that we're suddenly going to start having sex and I'm going to get her pregnant? That's not going to happen. I can't do this. Can she do this?

My mind is racing, trying to figure out if she can do what she says she can do. She probably can. Sasha has charisma for days and seems to know everyone. It wouldn't surprise me at all, given who her father is, that she has friends on the exam boards.

The wait staff of the restaurant is bringing the table champagne, and a glass of grapefruit juice for Sasha. After all, she is pregnant.

Somehow I manage to raise my glass and toast. But I can't speak. If I do the truth is going to come spilling out and I'm going to risk everything that I've ever worked for. My dad gives me a look, but I shake my head. I don't know what he'll do if I tell him the truth. He's so enamored by Dr. Pratt that he'll probably tell me to go along with it.

The fact that Dr. Pratt—Andrew—is one of the most influential doctors in the country has gotten way too far under his skin. I never should have gone along with this. What did I know? Dating the boss's daughter seemed like an okay way to make him like me. Now I feel like such a fucking idiot. Not only do I lose my career if I say anything now, but I lose his respect because I've been lying the whole time.

Shit.

What am I going to do?

The only place I want to be is with

Olivia. What am I going to tell her? How do I tell her? How do I get out of this mess?

Because I have to get out of this. I'm not going to be stuck with Sasha for the rest of my life because she's blackmailing me. I'll think of something. I have to.

I feel like I'm in a fog as Sasha loops her arm in mine and Dr. Pratt comes around the table to clap me on the back. My father is looking at me like I'm crazy, because he's noticed that I haven't said anything. I plaster a smile on my face because it's the only way I'll get out of here. I haven't heard a word that anyone's said either. Sasha could have said that we were moving to Hawaii and I wouldn't know.

I stammer out some words thanking Dr. Pratt for the lunch and his congratulations and make up something about having to get ready to go to the hospital. He's my boss, but he doesn't manage the residents. He won't know that I don't have to be there until midnight.

Sasha grabs me and forces a kiss onto my cheek, and I try not to shudder. I leave the restaurant, trying to keep my breathing under control. I want to scream and shout and punch something, but under all those thoughts is the one that keeps pulsing along with my heartbeat. Ollie. Ollie. Ollie.

If I can just get to Ollie, somehow this will all be okay. It has to be.

Please.

CHAPTER FOURTEEN

Ollie

I'm curled on the couch with a blanket and a book and the cutest lounge clothes I own when the doorbell rings. I know that it's Adam. He texted and said that he was on his way. Just his text gave me butterflies in my stomach, and I went out of way to make sure that I look good again. I mean, normal lounge clothes for me are ratty sweats that are so worn that they have comfort holes in them. Not tonight. Tonight I look cute and I'm practically holding my breath waiting for him to appear around the corner of the stairs. And then he does, and my breath is knocked out of me all over again.

He's not in his tux anymore, just simple jeans and t-shirt, which doesn't make him any less devastating. "Hi," I say.

Adam doesn't hesitate, pulling me into a kiss right there on the doorstep. I'm startled and god, I could live for surprises like these. The kiss reaches down into my gut and pulls, tugging pleasure and arousal through my whole body. The kiss seems almost desperate, like he's trying to convince himself that I'm real.

"Hi," he says, when he pulls away, leaving me dazed. "I missed you."

"Me too."

I pull him into the apartment and shut the door, noticing now that he has a messenger bag slung over his shoulder. "Are you planning on staying over again?" I really wouldn't mind that. In fact, I'd love it.

"I wish I could," he says, "but I have to be at the hospital at midnight."

"Oh." I try not to show my disappointment.

"But," he says, "I'm going to stay as long as I can." Adam slides his bag off his shoulder. "I kept my promise and brought you a present, but I want you to close your eyes."

"Ooookay," I say. I don't usually love surprises, due largely in part to the prom night incident, but I'll trust him this time. I go into the living room and sit on the couch again. If I'm going to have a surprise then I'm at least going to be comfortable while I do it.

I feel his weight on the couch next to

me, and he slips something into my hands. It's a book. All right, a book is a good surprise. But what book? "Can I open?"

"Yes."

I do, and...oh my god. I'm holding what must be the most beautiful edition of *World's Waterfall* that I've ever seen. The dust cover is embossed and has gold details and *wow*. "This is beautiful," I say. Flipping the cover open, my stomach does a little flip-flop. It's *signed*. I've always wanted a signed copy of these books, but I've never had a chance. The author is notoriously reclusive and almost never does signings. "How did you get this?"

His smile is tiny and infuriating. "I have my ways."

"This is amazing, I mean, what made

you think of this?"

Adam points to the bookshelf. "I saw those last night," he says. "And I remembered that you liked them in high school."

There's something in my chest and I'm not sure if it's pain or relief or something entirely different. "You remember that?"

"Of course I do," he says. "I remember a lot more than you probably think I do. Even if it's stuff you don't want to remember."

"Yeah."

He clears his throat. "It's why I asked about your life. I want to know about it, and I hope to god it was better than high school because almost everyone in that school let you down. Including me."

"Adam," I say. "That's not your

responsibility."

"I know, but I still want to know everything."

I hold the book to my chest—I don't want to let it go yet. "After college, Lorraine and I moved here together. We were roommates for a while, but eventually we each wanted our own space. It took a few years for me to get the job at my firm, and I worked some weird temp jobs, but I look back on those years happily, even if they were hard. I went through a lot of therapy. All in all I've had a good life."

He's slipped closer while I was talking, and I'm aware of the distance between us. "How are your parents?"

"You really want to talk about my

parents right now?" I ask, looking at his lips.

"I really want to know everything about you," he says, "but you're right. Maybe it can wait."

I put the book carefully down onto the coffee table, and then I'm kissing him. He kisses me back, lips crushing mine and god, I could kiss him forever. We collapse onto the couch together, tangled together just like we were last night, but this doesn't feel as charged. This feels deliciously comfortable and comforting. Adam's hand slips behind my neck, tipping my face closer to his so he can kiss me more deeply, and I feel myself growing wet and that growing need in my stomach that wants more of him and what we had last night and this morning.

Just like at the door, there's an edge to

Adam's kiss, and I suddenly remember where he just was. I pull back far enough for me to see his face, and I love that we're this close, pressed up against one another. "How did things go with your dad?"

Adam's face darkens. "As well as they ever go with him, I suppose."

"What happened?"

He doesn't say anything, but I feel like I watch a whole journey on his face. Pain and desperation and fear, and suddenly he focuses on me again, and it's like the rest of it disappears. "I'm sorry, I can't talk about it yet."

There's a tiny stab of disappointment, but I check it. It's hard to believe that this has been less than a day, but it has. I can't expect him to confide in me like that yet. "That's okay."

"Thank you," he kisses me softly and I melt against him. My shirt has ridden up and now his fingers are teasing my skin and it's driving me a little mad. "I'm going to be doing marathon shifts at the hospital for a few days. I'll be sleeping there. So I probably won't be able to see you, or call. I'll text when I can."

"That's okay," I say, laughing. "It's your job."

"I just didn't want you to think that I was disappearing."

I smile. "Thank you."

Leaning in, he presses his lips to my neck, tasting me with his tongue. "What were you doing before I got here?"

"Reading," I say. "Waiting for you."

"What were you reading?" His mouth is still on my skin, hands pushing my shirt up further so I'm more exposed.

I try to focus on the question, but he's making it very difficult. "A business book," I say. "So I can counsel my clients better."

He chuckles. "How very responsible of you."

"It's actually interesting."

"Tell me," he says, suddenly pulling me on top of him, and tugging at my shirt until I let him tug it off. Now I'm straddling him, looking down, and very much feeling how hard he is under my hips.

"Umm..." I'm not sure how I'm supposed to talk when all I can think about is fucking him. I can't remember any words. What are words? Why do they matter when this is happening?

Adam grins. "Go ahead."

"The book was about Parkinson's Law." He's undoing his belt, and my mouth goes dry. I stammer out the rest. "Which says that demand swells to meet supply."

"Isn't that backwards?"

"Not when you're talking about money," I say, transfixed by him and his hands as he grabs his cock and rolls on a condom. "Businesses get these infuses of money, and they justify reasons to spend it, and suddenly they have no cash flow."

"Fascinating," he says.

"Yeah."

"So," he tucks his fingers in the waistband of my pants and tugs them down. "Along with the book, I brought a very large box of condoms. Are you saying that the demand for them is going to swell to meet the supply I brought?"

I rise up just enough to let him slip into me, and I moan. "I think the demand for those was already there."

"Good," he says, thrusting up into me. From everything last night and this morning, I'm just a little sore, but the tiny edge of pain somehow makes the pleasure that much sharper. I close my eyes, letting it wash over me as we roll our hips together.

Lowering myself onto his chest, his arms come around me, holding me close while he moves faster, thrusts deeper, and I hold on, because it's perfect and my mind is blank and I don't think I can move even if I wanted to.

Adam groans as he moves, one thrust after another after another. My mouth is open in a silent cry, and I'm pulling in breath after breath, just trying to hold on, to feel. Yes, sweet god yes.

And then I'm on my back again. I'm not sure how I got there, but Adam is above me and I can't look away. There's something about this, I'm not sure what. I get why he didn't want to fuck on the couch last night, but doing it now feels *real* somehow. Like in this short time we went from being old acquaintances to lovers and to a real and actual couple. It's casual and breathtaking and I'm so close.

So close.

I take a breath and hold it, trying to make the moment before—the pleasure pulsing and spinning and shimmering—last. And then Adam drives in one more time and I can't hold it. Everything explodes in golden fireworks behind my eyes, and I shake underneath him. The orgasm is fast like an adrenaline rush that fizzes through me, and it feels like every nerve is overloaded at once, tingling up my spine and outward before evaporating and leaving me cursing under my breath.

Adam laughs, and then groans as he speeds up, so close too. I grab his face and kiss him, opening my mouth to him and showing him how much I loved that. I feel his breath catch and he pushes in once more, holding deep inside me. His cock jerks inside me as he comes, and he's kissing me hard, not letting me go.

I'm not sure how long it takes us to come back. It's a while, we're lost in each other and our kiss and the aftermath of pleasure.

Adam pulls away, standing and disappearing into the bathroom for a minute. I re-adjust my clothes, and when Adam comes back, he lies down next to me again, and wraps his arms around me.

"I'm so glad I bought a couch that's deep enough for two."

His lips are pressed against my forehead, and I feel the vibration when he laughs. "Me too." He breathes deep. "Ollie, I know it probably feels like ten years too late, but I like you."

I'm blushing even though he's not looking at my face.

"I really like you, and I want to make sure that you know. That you don't think I'm just using the opportunity for sex."

"I hadn't thought that," I say, "but I'm happy that you let me know. And I like you too. If I'm honest with myself, I don't think that I ever stopped liking you."

His hold tightens a little, and the tiny gesture warms my chest. "We're going to need to learn about each other as adults."

"What's your favorite color?" I ask, laughing. "Like that?"

"Blue, and yes, like that."

Leaning my forehead against his chest, I take a breath. "I like purple, but not the dark purple. More like periwinkle. I still love *World's Waterfall* even if it's nerdy. I want to travel way more than I have, somewhere amazing like Greece or Ireland or Sri Lanka. I do like my job, but I fantasize about quitting and being a writer who lives by the beach. I want a perfect wedding and kids someday, and no matter what I've eaten, I will always make room for pizza."

I can feel him smiling. "That's a good list."

"It's your turn."

He takes a moment, and he does start to speak his voice sounds different. Deeper, almost emotional. "I like my job, but sometimes I want to run away and never come back. But now, I'd take you with me."

"That sounds nice."

One of Adam's hands moves up and tangles in my hair, gently tugging on it until I tilt my face back to look up at him. "Maybe someday."

"Where would we go?" I ask him as he touches his lips to mine, barely a breath of a kiss.

"Anywhere. Those places you listed are great. We could go to Cape Cod. Or Hawaii and have a hut on the beach. We could go hiking and stay in a tent the whole time. Anywhere but here."

There's something too real in his voice. "Are you okay?"

"Of course," he says, but there's a flash

of pain in his eyes that he doesn't entirely hide, and I don't dare ask what it is. I can't push him for that. I don't have that right, yet.

"So," I say, changing the subject, putting on a smile. "You like me. I like you. You're not using me for sex. So what are we doing?"

"I want to know you," Adam says. "I want to date you. And, if after a few dates you decide you still like me, I have every intention of asking you to be my girlfriend. After that, who knows?"

My breath catches in my chest. In high school, there's almost nothing that I wouldn't have done to hear Adam say something like that. And it feels just as good, if not more, now. He wants *me*. He likes *me*.

"I like that plan," I say, yawning. I'm suddenly tired. "When do you have to leave?"

"Not for a while."

I shake myself a little. "I don't want to fall asleep. Not while you're here."

"Why not?" This smile is real and more like what I already recognize as the real Adam.

"Because you're here, and it still feels new and like we're on borrowed time."

He brushes the hair back from my face. "We're not on borrowed time. And if you're tired, you should sleep. I'll hold you for as long as I can."

The butterflies in my stomach are totally out of control right now, but the sudden burst of exhaustion is pulling me down, and Adam tucks me closer to his body.

His warmth is so good, and I fade into what feels like total and complete safety and comfort.

I don't know how long it is when I surface, Adam tucking a blanket around my body. He's crouched down by me and I reach out for his hand. "Don't go."

"Believe me, I don't want to." He kisses me softly. "But I have to. I'll see you soon."

"Promise?"

"Promise." He finishes arranging the blanket around me, and I hear his footsteps leaving as I fade back to sleep.

CHAPTER FIFTEEN

Ollie

Adam doesn't text the next day. Or the next. I start to get nervous because even though he said all those nice things, that was right after we'd had sex and he was happy. Who knows, maybe he didn't mean it? My gut tells me he wasn't lying but I can't make ten years of anxiety just evaporate.

I text Lorraine and all she texts back is an eye-roll emoji. Then,

Girl, that boy is so hooked on you, I can't believe you'd even think that.

He isn't hooked on me.

Yes he fucking is. And don't argue with me.

It's my turn to roll my eyes, and I put my phone down only to hear it buzz again.

If you're worried, why don't you bring him lunch or something? Medical students eat like shit while they're on these kinds of shifts. Plus, you'd get to see him?

I mean...that could work?

What if he doesn't want me showing up at work?

If he doesn't, then that's not exactly a good sign. Like he wants you to keep you a secret. If you're really worried, then this is a good solution. It will tell you what he's thinking.

I don't really like the idea of testing him when he doesn't know what's happening.

I mean, you're not doing it as a test, you want to see him right?

Yeah, of course.

Well, then go see him. It's just a side effect that his reaction to you will show you a lot about

233

where you stand.

I suppose that's true.

It is. Go get him.

It's almost the end of the workday, and I'm basically killing time anyway. My boss knows that I do my work and get it done, so he doesn't care when I come and go. He trusts that whatever I need to do is in good hands.

I double-check that everything is taken care of before packing up. I honestly have no idea what Adam likes to eat, but I'm going to take a chance and pick up some pasta from one of my favorite places. Pasta seems like a safe choice. Most people like pasta, right? Besides, it has to be better than hospital food either way.

For a second I debate going home to change out of my really boring work clothes, but I'm way closer to the hospital here at work. Going all the way back to Astoria and coming back to Manhattan would easily take more than an hour, and I don't want to waste that kind of time.

I place the order for the food before I head out the door. This is one of my go-tos for lunch when I forget to pack one. They're fast and delicious without being overly expensive. When you find those qualities in a restaurant in New York, it's kind of like spotting a unicorn.

When I walk in the door ten minutes

later, my food is already packed and waiting, and it takes me less than five minutes to pay and get out. Now that I'm committing, I feel a buzz of excitement in my stomach. There's a small part of me that thinks I should text him first, but fuck it, I want to surprise him. And I definitely want to see how hot he looks in scrubs.

I take a cab to the Upper East Side, not wanting to deal with rush-hour delays on the subway. There's still a bit of traffic, but I think it's faster. I have the cab drop me off at the main entrance to the hospital. Now I just have to figure out where exactly the pediatrics department is.

A friendly woman at the front desk gives me directions, and I follow them as best I can through a maze of hallways and a couple of elevators. I know that I've found the right place when the elevator doors open and there's a giant bulletin board filled with children's drawings right in front of the door.

It's still very maze-like, but I find my way to a nurse's station. "Hi," I say to the woman dressed in pale pink scrubs. "I'm looking for Dr. Carlisle."

"Are you the mother of a patient?" she asks.

"No," I say, blushing despite the fact that I have no reason. "I'm...uhhh...I brought him dinner."

She smiles then. "Oh you must be the girlfriend. I'll page him for you."

The girlfriend. He's already told people about me? Something about that gives me a little twinge of happiness. She speaks into the phone, paging him to the nurse's station and I wait, biting my lip with nervousness.

He comes around the corner, and damn, scrubs are a good look for him. He could be a doctor from a TV medical drama with how hot he looks. The dark blue sets off his tan skin and blue eyes. It takes him a second to see me, but when he does, he breaks into a huge smile. "What are you doing here?"

"I brought you food," I say.

Adams eyes go wide. "Seriously?"

"Seriously."

He laughs, pulling me in for a quick kiss. "You're a lifesaver. Now I don't have to eat from the vending machine."

"You guys don't have a cafeteria?" I ask as he takes my hand and guides us away from the nursing station.

"We do, but trust me, you don't want to eat there. I do it as little as possible. But we'll go there now, cause it's the easiest place to eat."

I squeeze his hand. "I'm not interrupting anything?"

"You actually came at a really good time. Visiting hours are almost over and I have to do my rounds in a little while. But I can play hooky for a while."

"I'm glad," I say. "I was nervous you wouldn't be happy with me just showing up. But I wanted to see you."

Adam lets go of my hand, instead

wrapping his arm around my hips as we walk. "This was an amazing surprise. I haven't been able to get you out of my head, and I'm sorry I haven't been able to text."

We take a set of stairs down one floor and through a set of double doors to a sterile white room filled with tables and chairs and a really depressing looking food line. "So what are we having?" he asks as we grab a table off to the side.

I hand him the bag. "I didn't know what you liked, so I thought that pasta was a safe bet."

He sticks his face in the bag and groans. "It's an amazing bet. I love Italian and this smells fucking amazing. Thank you."

I help him get the take-out containers

out of the bag and he steps away from the table to grab some plates and silverware. "Where on earth did you get this?" he asks. "It's really good."

I tell him about my unicorn Italian place and I think I may have a new convert on my hands.

"I wonder if I tip them really well if they'll deliver up here," he says.

"Never know unless you try. And if they don't, I can sometimes be your delivery service."

Adam smiles. "I'd like that."

"How are things here?"

His face falls a bit. "They've been a bit crazy. We had some transfer cases that have all hands on deck. Just some really sick kids.

We're doing everything we can, but it's touch and go at the moment."

I reach across the table and take his hand. "I'm sorry."

"Don't be. It's not your fault. But we've all been running around a little more than normal. Which is why I haven't texted. I wanted to."

I shake my head. "Don't worry, I get it."

"As soon as I get out of here on Thursday I want to take you out."

"You're done with your shifts then?"

He nods, taking another bite of spaghetti and sauce. "Yes, and if you're not sick of it, I have an Italian restaurant of my own that I'd love to take you to."

"Which one?"

"Del Posto."

I try to keep my mouth from falling open. Del Posto is an amazing restaurant in lower Manhattan near the river. I've know it's amazing because it's expensive and exclusive.

Adam smiles when he sees my face. "What?"

"You can get into Del Posto?"

"Sure."

I shake my head. "That's...insane."

"But you want to go?"

"Yes, of course I want to go!" I say it a little too loudly and suddenly I'm looking around to make sure I didn't startle any sick people. "I can't believe that's where you want to take me. It's going to be way better than this," I gesture to our food.

"Seriously, Ollie," he says, "this is amazing. You saved me from having Cheez-Its for dinner."

I smile. "Okay."

"Come visit me whenever you want. I can't promise that I'll be free, but I'll always try to come say hi." He lowers his voice, "And if I have time, there's more than that I'll do."

"Oh?" I ask. "Do tell."

CHAPTER SIXTEEN

Adam

I can't believe she's here. The past two days I've barely had a chance to breathe, and every time I run into Dr. Pratt, he smiles at me like an idiot and I sink a little lower. I've wanted to talk to Ollie, to hold her, anything, but I've barely been able to eat. The fact that she brought me food without even asking, it makes my chest ache. This is what I've been missing.

Sasha has never done anything like this in our entire time being "together." If she really cared, you might think that she would show it. Or at least pretend. And that's why we're not together. And why Ollie is sitting across from me with that coy little smile on her face. I like the way her hair is falling into her eyes and the way the buttons on her shirt are a little too tight. I shift in my chair because I'm getting hard and I can't actually take her on top of a table in the cafeteria even if I desperately want to.

Her eyes are sparkling with mischief, and suddenly I'm not hungry for more food. I glance on my watch. I still have a little time. "I could show you, if you wanted."

She clears away what little is left of the food into the nearest trashcan and I take her back upstairs and to one of the on-call rooms. I glance both ways just to make sure that Dr. Pratt isn't around before we slip inside and I lock the door.

"I swore this only happened on TV," she says.

"You'd be surprised at the amount of drama from those shows that's pretty close to reality," I say, loving the way her face lights up like she's just won a prize.

"I like you in scrubs," she says, voice suddenly low and intense. And I'm frozen in place because Ollie's on her knees and has my pants down and her mouth on me before I can blink. I sink back against the door, overwhelmed by the heat of her mouth oh my cock. "Shit, Ollie."

She hums, and god, the way that feels makes me want to lose it. But I'm not going to. Not yet.

She teases me with her tongue, swirling around the tip of my cock and licking downward and back up. I can't breathe because *damn* it feels good.

My whole body is tense. Just the fact that Ollie is here and willing to do this is enough to make me come, and the only way I'm going to last is gritting my teeth and hanging on as long as I can.

Ollie rises up on her knees, and dives down onto my cock. The sound that comes from my throat is barely human, but I can't help it. I'm sheathed in soft, perfect heat, and she's sucking me like it's the one thing she was made to do. I hit her throat and I clench my jaw. I'm not small, and she has almost all of me inside. Holy fuck.

I look down and see her lips wrapped

around me, and my cock jerks. It's one of the hottest things I've ever seen. Then she looks up, and Ollie's green eyes on mine, mouth stretched on my cock. Oh my god.

She sucks back up my shaft and dives down again and I can't hold on. "Ollie," I manage, just a second before pleasure shoots from my balls into my cock and up into my spine. Waves of warmth and pleasure rocket through me, so intense I lose my vision. And through it I can still feel Ollie sucking.

"Jesus, Ollie," I say, bracing myself on the door. She grins at me, giving my cock a saucy lick before I pull her off her knees and onto the bed. "Food and you," I say. "This really was the best surprise I could have asked for."

She giggles and the happiness in that

sound gets under my skin, and for a second I don't feel like everything is hopeless. Like maybe we can actually have this.

I undo the buttons on her shirt one at a time, kissing every inch of skin that I reveal. I like the way I can hear her little gasps as I kiss her, like every touch is a shock.

The bra she's wearing is simple and black, and that's just as sexy as wearing lingerie because I know this was spur of the moment for her. She decided to come see me and she came as she was, she didn't think she needed to dress up or do anything different, and I love that.

Ollie moans softly as I play with her breasts. I've never known a woman who gets so turned on by this and it makes me hard again. I've never done this in an on-call room before, though I know plenty of others who have.

Dipping down, I trace her belly button with my tongue, and my hand is on the zipper of her pants when there's a knock on the door, and the handle rattles. "Dr. Carlisle?"

It's Darcy, the nurse on duty. Shit. "Yes?"

"You're needed in the PICU."

"I'll be right there." I rest my head on Ollie's stomach. "I'm sorry, I have to go."

She sits up, quickly buttoning her shirt, and there's a blush on her face. She's embarrassed. "It's okay."

I tilt her face up to mine and kiss her, deep as I can for the moment I can spare. "I owe you several orgasms and one amazing

251

Italian dinner."

"Yes, you do," she says, grinning.

"I'll text you tonight, okay?"

"Okay."

I press my lips to hers one final time before adjusting my clothes and jogging out of the room. A PICU call is one that I can't ignore. I didn't hear them page me on the overhead and they didn't actually page me— probably because Darcy already knew where I was. I'm hoping it's something that I can help, and that I'm not too late.

***

Thankfully the call wasn't an

emergency, even though all PICU calls are treated that way as a matter of course. One of our kids had thrown up. He's already too small and the vomit could be a sign of something worse, but I think it's just an upset stomach. None of his other vitals are in bad shape. I'm doing tests just to be safe.

I told the parents and now I'm heading to the locker room to get my phone. I'm keeping my word that I'm going to text Ollie tonight. Who knows, maybe I can convince her to send me some pictures. I wasn't finished with her, and that unfinished business is now rising in my pants.

"Adam!"

A chill goes down my spine, and I turn to find Sasha and her father walking down the hallway toward me. She waves enthusiastically.

I wait for them to catch up to me. "Hello," I say, letting her kiss my cheek. It's the one thing I'll let her do.

Dr. Pratt's hand lands on my shoulder. "Sasha came by to say hello and tell me that your first sonogram is next week."

I look at Sasha. "I didn't know that."

"Yep!" she says. "All scheduled."

"I'll let you two have a moment alone," Dr. Pratt says. "Adam, meet me for rounds when you're finished."

"Yes, sir."

I wait until he's around the corner before I turn on Sasha. "A sonogram? How exactly are you going to explain to the technician that you are completely *not with child*?"

She waves a hand. "It will be fine. I'll have a tragic miscarriage before then."

"Do you know anything about pregnancy or did you just read the cover of a magazine? You're barely at the stage where you can tell you're pregnant. How exactly are you going to pull off knowing that you had a miscarriage? Not to mention the fact that you're treating something very painful for a lot of people like it doesn't mean anything."

She looks at me, and her eyes narrow. "The only thing that means anything is that you and I are together, and we're going to stay that way. I know you don't see it that way, but trust me, it's for your own good. You may not see it now, but you will."

"Fuck off, Sasha."

Slipping closer to me, her face softens, and I've seen that face before when she's going to try to get what she wants. "I see you're having a little bit of a problem," she says, glancing down at my pants. "I can help you with that."

She reaches for me, and I catch her by the wrist. "Don't ever touch me. You're blackmailing me into being with you. What makes you think I would *ever* let you touch me?"

Sasha pouts. "Come on, Adam. What can you possibly see in that slut that I don't have?"

"Maybe the fact that even though you've tried to ruin her life multiple times, she would never call you a slut." I turn and walk away from her, not looking back. Jesus, I need to get out of this mess, but I still don't know how.

I make it to the locker room without another interruption, and grab my phone. It's time for me to get a few hours of sleep, and for me to text Ollie.

CHAPTER SEVENTEEN

Ollie

I've barely gotten home when my phone buzzes in my pocket. I'm smiling before I even see the screen.

I told you that I would text you.

I'm glad you did.

I pause before sending another message.

Is everything okay? PICU?

Yes, thankfully it wasn't a real emergency. Now I get to take a nap, or...

Or...?

I unlock my door and go inside, and suddenly the phone rings. I look at the screen, and it's Adam video calling me. I hit the green button as I lock the door behind me, and Adam's face appears. He's smiling, lying down on a bed which I'm pretty sure is the same bed we almost had sex on. "Long time no see," I say.

"I see you're home."

"You are correct." I drop my purse and kick off my shoes and walk with him into my bedroom. "And you still haven't told me what you meant by 'or...'"

He stretches, putting one of his arms behind his head and I'm distracted by the way that position shows off the muscles in his arm. "I thought my calling might have been an indication."

What he means suddenly hits me, and I freeze. "Oh." I blink. "I've never done that before."

"If you don't want to, that's fine."

"No," I say, "I want to." God, I want to. I want to see him as much as I can, and I was disappointed that we were interrupted, even though I would never stop him from doing his job. "I just, don't know what to do."

"This time," he says, voice low, "I'll tell you what to do."

The way his voice cuts through the silence in my room, everything I felt in that little room comes rushing back and I'm ready.

"There will be a next time?"

He grins, "I still have a year of this ahead of me, and as much as I wish that I could sneak you in here for sex every night, I don't think that would work."

"No, probably not."

His face suddenly goes serious and sexy. "Unbutton your shirt."

My stomach drops. "Now?"

"Now."

"You don't know if I live alone, you know. You never asked."

Adam raises an eyebrow. "Do you live alone?"

"Yes."

"Are you nervous?"

I swallow. "Yes."

"Why?"

"I don't know."

"Olivia," he says, and the way his voice caresses my name makes me shiver. "I've touched you. I've tasted you. My tongue, fingers, and cock have all been inside you. My cock has been in your mouth. I've sucked on your breasts. All of that happened without a camera in-between us."

My face flames red, and I close my eyes because I'm embarrassed and incredibly aroused at the same time. "It's different."

"It's not." There's a rustling, and I open my eyes to see that he's taken off his shirt. "I'm going first." His free hand dips below the scope of the camera and there's more rustling. "See? Now I'm naked."

He slowly and pointedly pans the camera down his body and I take in his abs and legs and his very erect cock.

"I'm not sure I did a good enough job taking care of you if you're still that hard."

"That's not true," he says. "I just didn't have enough of you."

I meet his eyes through the camera, and there's a pull in my chest and my gut, and there's a feeling that this is more than what we both thought.

"I don't think I'll ever have enough of you," he says softly.

There's a silence that hangs between us, like something big is begging to be said, but it can't be. Not while we're chatting like this. Adam clears his throat. "Unbutton your shirt, Ollie."

I do, and suddenly I laugh. "This is harder than I thought with one hand."

"I'll buy you a little stand for your phone."

"I'll be your own personal cam girl?"

"Something like that, yeah." I get my shirt unbuttoned and go to shrug it off my shoulders. "No," he says, "Not yet."

I stop. "Why?"

"You're nervous," he says. "So I want you to do exactly what I say, and nothing else."

My stomach drops again, and the heat from my blush shifts downward. "Okay."

"Put down the phone, take off your pants and your bra. Leave your panties on and your shirt unbuttoned."

My pussy clenches, and I'm not sure why him instructing me to take off my clothes is so hot, but it is. I can feel the slickness gathering between my legs, and I press them together in an attempt to stop my arousal from growing. It doesn't work.

I get back on the bed and lay back, breathing for a second before I pick up the phone again. In the little camera that shows me, I see what he sees. Oh. The two sides of my shirt are barely covering my breasts, and it's sexy. He knows what he's doing.

Adam groans. "You look good, baby."

"I feel good."

His free hand drops out of the shot again, and I know that he's touching himself. God, it's sexy knowing that. Slowly, I can feel my anxiety about this dropping away.

"Are your nipples hard?"

They are. They always are when I'm aroused. Now that I think about it, they basically get hard whenever I'm within a few feet of Adam. I nod.

"Show me."

I pull back one side of my shirt, and

then the other, so that the fabric falls on either side of me and I'm completely bared to him. There's something breathless and exciting about it. He's seen me before, but not like this.

"Touch them. Touch them like I would touch them."

My anxiety surges again, and I hesitantly lift my hands to my nipple. I've done this plenty of times alone, but with him watching..."Ollie, close your eyes."

I do.

"Touch yourself."

Drawing my fingers across my skin, I feel the little goosebumps that form after my fingers leave. With my eyes closed, it's easier to pretend that he's here and I'm not the one touching myself. I circle my nipple, slowly rolling it between my thumb and forefinger and tugging. My body responds the way it always does, with heat and wetness and wanting more.

"Switch," he says softly, and I do, working my other nipple until they're both so hard and sensitive that just the stirring of air from my fan is making shiver.

"God, I love your tits," he says with a groan. "I want to fuck them."

I moan. That image turns me on. I want to feel his cock sliding between my breasts. I know he'll come and I sure will. "Yes," I say. "Please."

"I'm going to," he says. "I'm going to straddle you and fuck your tits until we both come."

The pressure is building in my core and I switch my hand back to my other breast without him telling me to, but I need it. I need it.

I'm pulling harder now, god, I wish Adam were here. I need his mouth on me, I need him to suck and lick and I throw my memory back to that night and I imagine the feeling while I toy with my nipples, and I'm so close, and—

"Stop."

Adam's voice penetrates the haze in my brain. "Ollie, stop."

"Why?" I gasp, barely able to pull my hand away from myself.

The pleasure that was building fades a

little, until it's manageable. I open my eyes and see him, staring at me, I can feel the lust and the need even through the camera.

"Trust me," he says.

I put my hand down by my side, trying to catch my breath. Adam's arm is moving, and he lowers the camera so I can see his cock and his hand stroking it. "See how much I like watching you?" he asks. The tip of his cock is glistening, and I can see the sheen of sweat on his skin when he brings the camera back to his face.

"You stopped me."

"I did."

"Why?" I ask again.

"Because now I want your hand in your panties and your fingers on your clit and I want you to show me."

At this point I don't think I should be able to blush, but the way he says it, so blunt and open has the blood rising to my chest and face but I still find myself putting my hand between my legs. The minute I touch my clit every bit of arousal floods back like fire, and I aim the camera downward, though I know not much is visible.

"Good. Look at me."

I bring the camera back up to my face, but I don't stop moving my fingers. "I can't stop," I tell him.

"Don't." he says. "Keep going. Come with me."

I close my eyes, and I let go, moving my fingers, drawing the pleasure up and out in the way I know works best, and within a minute I'm so close that I'm arching backwards on the bed. And suddenly it's there, I cry out, loud in my empty apartment, coming on my hand and oh god shit yes fuck.

"Yes, Ollie," Adam moans, and his breath is ragged as he comes too.

I let the orgasm go, let it flow through me, making me shake and go blind for a few seconds before my body goes limp, sated.

"Adam," I say.

"Olivia."

I laugh breathlessly. "That was good."

"Yes, it was," he says. "Just one of several orgasms I owe you."

Rolling over on my side, I prop myself up on my elbow which drapes my shirt in a flirtatious and scandalous way. "Well I'm looking forward to the rest of them."

"Me too," he says, yawning. "But I should get sleep. If not, I'm going to be dead on my feet in a few hours."

"Will you text me tomorrow?"

"I will," he says, "and you make sure you're ready for Thursday. I'm picking you up and taking you out."

"Okay." I can't keep the smile off my face.

"Okay."

He's smiling too, and there's some empty air where we're both smiling each other and neither of us wants to hang up. "Good night, Ollie."

"Good night, Adam."

He ends the call and I immediately pull up a text message to Lorraine.

Girl, I have some stuff to tell you.

CHAPTER EIGHTEEN

Ollie

I step into the coffee shop and find Lorraine waving me down. She's already ordered me a chai and I sink into the seat across from her gratefully.

"I don't have super long," I say. "I left early yesterday to go to the hospital, so shorter lunch today."

"That's fine," she says, watching me take a sip of the chai. "But I need *details* sister, I'm not going to forgive you for not texting me everything if you don't give me some details!"

I laugh, nearly choking on my drink. "What do you want to know?"

"Everything!" she says way too loudly. "How did it go at the hospital? What happened after?"

I can't stop laughing, but I manage to tell her everything—sparing the dirtiest of details because I'm still not used to this and I'm not about to tell her the size of Adam's cock or just how far I managed to get it down my throat.

But by the end of the story Lorraine's jaw is hanging open. "I am seriously impressed, Ollie."

"Why?"

"Because this is so unlike you! Let's face it, we both know I'm the slutty one in the friendship. And now you're sleeping with people and having phone sex and–oh my god–I'm so happy I'm rubbing off on you."

I can't stop laughing and I can't breathe. "Stop it. You're not rubbing off on me."

"I totally am. You'll thank me later."

"Can you hook me up for tomorrow though?" I ask. I hate asking for her help again in the dress department but I'm just not that fancy and I don't own anything pretty enough for Del Posto.

"Of course, you know I've got you."

Which is how I end up back in the Bergdorf's make-up chair on Thursday afternoon with Maren doing my make-up. "This time," she says, waving my eyes closed, "we're going full on sexy. Smoky eyes, dark lips. He's not going to be able to take his eyes off you."

Or his hands, I finish in my head.

When I open my eyes again, I barely recognize myself. I look like someone who should be on a red carpet, not...*me*.

"Maren," I say. "You're a miracle worker."

She sticks her tongue out. "I know."

Lor is waiting for me in the dressing room. "Okay, I've got the perfect thing." She pulls a dress of the rack with a flourish. It's a deep purple color, deeper than I usually like but it's *gorgeous* in this dress. Immediately I know that I want to try it on.

I'll never understand how Lorraine has

such an eye for this. "I just need you to pick out all my clothes, all the time," I tell her through the curtain.

"Name the day, girlfriend. You know that I've been dying to get my hands on your wardrobe."

The dress has an off-the-shoulder neckline and a skinny waist with a flouncy skirt that ends at my knees. It feels like something out of the 1950s with a modern flare. It's absolutely perfect. I push the curtain back. "This is amazing. You've got shoes?"

She hands me a pair of black and purple heels, and I slip them on and stand on the same pedestal I stood barely a week ago. Stunning! "I don't know how you do it, Lor."

"I'm magic."

"Yes, you are, and I owe you one."

"Girl, as long as you get some you don't owe me a damn thing."

I laugh. "I still haven't sent you the box of chocolates for last week."

"Chocolate doesn't have an expiration date, and I'm always accepting. So no worries." She tugs me down off the pedestal. "Now get going or you're going to be late and I'm not going to have all my amazing work ruined by a late entrance."

I roll my eyes. "Fine. I love you."

"Love you too, bitch! Go get some ass." She waves as she heads back to her department. I know she still has some clients to see today, so I'm grateful that she had time to work with me.

There's no way I'm getting on the subway and potentially ruining all of their hard work, so I catch a cab back to my apartment. I'm just on time to get back upstairs and pretend that all this magic was made by myself, though I'll gladly spread the gospel of Lorraine if given a chance.

I'm too nervous and excited to sit down or relax, so I make myself a cup of tea in the kitchen, slipping off the heels until I absolutely need them.

It's not long. Adam is punctual, and he rings the doorbell a couple minutes before he was supposed to arrive. I buzz him up, but this time I don't open the door and wait. Lorraine put in the work, and I'm going to give it the grand reveal that it deserves.

I stay in the kitchen until he knocks,

and then I answer the door. The way his face goes slack and his eyes go dark as they take me in is totally, totally worth it. "Ollie," he says, and everything on his face says that he's awed and impressed.

I've never seen anyone look at me that way before. I like it.

"Hi."

"You look amazing."

"Thank you."

I step aside and he comes in, never taking his eyes off me. Maren was right. And now I get the chance to look at him. He looks predictably amazing in a suit that was clearly tailored for him. It has a soft sheen to it that makes it almost shimmer in the light, and he looks like he stepped out of a magazine ad.

Then again, thanks to Maren and Lorraine, so do I. We make quite the pair tonight.

"Am I allowed to kiss you in that make-up?"

"You're allowed to kiss me anytime," I say, "Make-up be damned."

"Good," he says, pulling me in for a kiss that makes my knees go weak. "I missed you."

It doesn't feel like we've been apart long enough to be missed, but I know what he's saying. This feels good, being together. "Yeah," I say. "Me too." I grab my little purse off the kitchen counter. "Should we go?"

Adam smiles. "We have a little time, and I need to take care of something first."

"What?"

"Something I owe you."

I don't understand, and then I do, because Adam is kneeling in front of me, gathering my skirts and pushing them aside so his head is between my legs. I'm wearing a lacy thong that Lorraine gave me for under the dress, and Adam's tongue run across the tiny patch of fabric. "Adam," I gasp. "What are you doing?"

He doesn't say anything, but pushes the thong aside and seals his mouth over my clit, sucking it deep and hard, and I have to brace myself against the wall, just like he did in the hospital. Oh god, of course.

Adam's mouth is hard and insistent, stroking me with his tongue in long steady strokes that are bringing me higher, arousing me faster than anything I thought possible.

284

Just when I think I'm about to break, he changes his pattern, moving down and sliding inside me, stroking again and again and then back up to swirl and suck and graze his teeth against me.

I'm balanced on my heels and against the wall and I don't know how he's so fucking good at this. Little strokes now, faster and faster and focused on my clit. There's pressure building and I'm resisting the urge to hike up my dress and grab his head and push him closer. Adam sucks one more time, and I tip over the edge, a swirling storm of pleasure spiraling up and out from my clit, and my legs nearly give out. I can't breathe or see, just feel his tongue on me, continuing this pleasure. It blows through me and leaves me new and fresh and finished.

"God," I say, sinking further against the wall.

One final, long lick across my pussy and Adam replaces my thong and then he's out from under my dress, smirking at me.

"I did tell you that I owed you orgasms."

"I know," I say. "I just...wasn't expecting that."

He braces his arms on either side of me, pressing close. "I don't think pleasure is a thing that should happen only when you expect it," he says. "And I plan on trying to give you as much unexpected pleasure as I can."

"Okay." I can't pretend that I'm mad about that.

"Now," he says, "We can go."

CHAPTER NINETEEN

Adam

Del Posto isn't a place that I've been a whole lot, but it's owned by some family friends so I know I can get a reservation when I need one. I hold Ollie's hand in the cab ride to the restaurant, and it feels so natural that I don't want to let go. She looks fucking fantastic, even better when she had the flush of the orgasm that I gave her.

I'm tempted to ravish her in the back of the cab, but despite our little sexual encounter in her foyer, tonight isn't about that. I want to talk to her. Listen to her. I want to know her for who she is now and not for who I remember her in high school. I want to show her that it's not just sex that I want. I want so much more than that.

We're lucky that the weather is pretty perfect today. T the sun is beginning to set when we pull up to the front of the restaurant, which is perfect because I know exactly where we're sitting. The view is going to be gorgeous.

I help her out of the cab, and I love just watching her. Ollie has such pure reactions to things. I feel like I'm reading a book whenever I look at her face, and I just want to keep reading. She's looking at the restaurant with a mix of awe and excitement, and if she's this psyched about the outside, she's going to lose her mind when she actually tastes the food.

"I still can't believe we're going here."

"The owner is a family friend," I say.

She shakes her head in disbelief. "Good friends to have."

"Yeah, I suppose so." I take her hand again, and we enter the restaurant. "Carlisle," I say to the hostess, and we don't have to wait at all. We're led back to one of their more private tables on a balcony that overlooks the Hudson River, and the breeze off the water is the perfect antidote to the remaining afternoon heat. I pull out Ollie's chair and she sits, her dress puffing out beneath her.

I have an image in my head of us sinking into bed together, and fucking her while surrounded by all those layers of skirt. I wonder if I can make that happen later tonight.

Sitting across from her, the light is streaming from behind her and it's such a perfect picture that I pull out my phone. "I need a picture of this," I say.

"Why?"

"Because the lighting is perfect, and I need a picture of you for my long and lonely nights at the hospital."

Ollie blushes, and I snap the picture right as she looks away toward the river. It's perfect. Gorgeous. A person is suddenly by our table, and I look up. "Anton," I say, "hello." I stand and hug him. "I didn't know you would be here tonight."

"When you called for a reservation, I

thought it had been so long that I needed to see you and say hello." He looks over at Ollie. "And who is your lovely companion?"

"This is Olivia Mitchell."

He holds out a hand and she takes it. "It's nice to meet you, Olivia Mitchell. I hope you know that you have an excellent young man here."

"I do know that," she says, smiling.

Anton turns back to me. "Tonight you're getting the chef's finest. I'll make sure they take care of you."

I shake his hand. "I appreciate that. Next time I come, you and I will have a drink."

"I'll hold you to that." Nodding to Ollie, he says, "It was lovely to meet you."

"You too," she says.

And then he's gone as quickly as he appeared. "Anton never stops moving," I say. "He's always chatting with patrons and his friends and sometimes he cooks too. He cares more about this restaurant and food more than any person I've ever met."

"He seems nice," she says, laughing. "From the thirty seconds he was here."

"He is, and if he says that he's making sure our food is amazing, it will be."

Our waiter appears with wine, and pours us each a glass. "So," she says, "you have a couple days off now?"

"I do, and I was actually going to ask you about that."

Ollie makes a sarcastic face. "You were

going to ask me about your days off?"

"In a way, yes."

"Okay?"

"I actually have two things that I need to ask you." I take a sip of wine ad clear my throat. "I was wondering if you wanted to go away this weekend. My family has a house out on the island. No one is there, and I want to just—"

"Yes," she says. "Hell yes. Did you think I would say no?"

"I mean, I know it's fast."

She shakes her head, and the sun catches her hair, distracting me. "Seriously, I'd love to." Then she lowers her voice. "We can't seem to keep our hands off each other, and a big house where we're all alone seems like the perfect place to get some of that out of our system."

I grin. "My thoughts exactly."

"What's the second thing?"

I sigh, this one is trickier. "My mother is hosting a party next week. I'd like you to come."

"You don't sound as happy about that one."

"I'm not," I say. "Though that has nothing to do with you. I generally don't love my parents' parties. Imagine all the parents of the people in our class and you have the people that populate those circles."

"Oh."

I laugh. "Yeah. It's a real fun time."

Ollie spins her wineglass on the table, and watches the watery reflection of light on the table. The truth is, I don't know how I'll be able to get myself out of my predicament by the party, but if worse comes to worse, I want Ollie to be there. But I need some way to warn her about what might happen if she goes. How can I tell her about Sasha without breaking her heart all over again? That's the last thing that I want, especially since what we have is so new and so good. I don't want to break it.

"Hey," Ollie says gently. "Where'd you go?"

"Sorry."

She reaches across the table and grabs my hand. "You have nothing to be sorry for. But you can tell me what's wrong."

How can I? "I'm not sure how."

"Is it a problem at work?"

"Kind of," I sigh. "I…agreed to something a few years ago that I thought would help my career. But it wasn't the right choice to make. It's kind of so obvious now that I'm not sure how I didn't see it then. But because of that choice, there's a couple people, my father included, who are making it hard to get off that path."

"Did it help?"

"My career?" She nods. "Maybe. I think I probably could have done just fine on my own."

She takes another sip of her wine, the breeze catching her hair and blowing it into her eyes for a second while she looks at the river. "And you can't…get out of this?"

"I'm trying."

The way she's looking at me, searching, it's like I can feel her stare in my chest. "What's stopping you?"

"I'm not sure that doing what I did helped my career, but it's made clear to me that reversing it would definitely hurt it."

Ollie frowns. "And you can't tell me what it is? Maybe I could help."

I brush my thumb across the back of her hand. "I wish I could," I say, and I really do. "But I can't right now."

"I'm sorry," she says, trying to pull her hand away. "I shouldn't have asked."

I don't let her pull away. "Of course you should have. Believe me, this would be easier if I could just talk about it. Hopefully soon I'll be able to."

She smiles, and it's a little sad. "Well I'm sorry that you have to deal with it at all."

"Me too."

I look out over the river for a second, and then back at Ollie. My eyes follow the line of her dress, and I'm distracted by her collarbones, sweeping gracefully out to her shoulders. "So… is Italian your favorite?" I say, asking a question to try to change the subject and bring back the lighthearted feeling that got lost in me almost admitting everything.

"Yeah," she says. "I love Italian. I think my second favorite is probably traditional American diner food. I can really go for a burger now and then." Our waiter appears with the first course, what looks like a small portion of artisanal fettuccine Alfredo, and Ollie grins. "But yeah, Italian is my favorite."

"It's my favorite too," I say. "Though I can always go for Thai too."

"Mmm." She groans as she takes a bite the pasta. "This is amazing. And so is Thai."

I take my own bite, and she's right. The pasta is creamy with the right proportion of pasta and sauce. Anton really has a talented chef here. I have to make sure that I tell him that the next time I see him.

"Now you can tell me about your parents," I say.

She laughs. "They're fine. They still live in the same house, still have the same routines. I think you'd like them."

"I'm sure I would."

She shakes her head. "They're definitely not in the same circles as your parents."

"I think that probably ensures that I'll like them more."

"Maybe," she laughs. "They'll do their best to embarrass me when you meet them. Be forewarned."

"If I get to see you blush more, it works in my favor."

At my comment, she blushes, and just like that, our magic is back. We fall back into the get-to-know-you game, and it's easier to forget the little blip. I wish I could confide in Ollie, I wish that I'd had the strength to say no when my father insisted. I wish that it were anyone but *Sasha* that was the problem. If it were anyone but her, this would be so much easier.

But it's not.

And I can't let tonight be about that. If I let it take over my mind, I'll go mad with guilt and I'll end up exploding the nuclear bomb that is my life. So I focus on Ollie and how beautiful she is, and everything that I'm learning about her.

She's an only child, which I knew. Her parents moved out of the city to rural Pennsylvania to retire. Her favorite vacation spot is the beach, any beach, and besides her love of *World's Waterfall*, she's also hugely and nerdily obsessed with origami. I didn't see any at her apartment, but then I wasn't looking for it.

I tell her about medical school and some of the crazy shenanigans that my friends and I got into while we were there. I tell her the story of how we played a prank on one of our teachers using a live goldfish, and the story of how I nearly broke my spine out of stupidity.

We laugh together, and drink wine, and by the time all of the five courses have passed we're both stuffed with delicious Italian food and just drunk enough that everything is perfect and glowing and happy. "My place?" I ask as we exit the restaurant into the gathering cool of evening.

"Yes," she says, pulling me down for a kiss in the middle of the street.

And that's that.

CHAPTER TWENTY

Ollie

I knew that Adam and his family were rich, but wasn't expecting the absolutely gorgeous apartment building that the cab lets us out in front of on the Upper West Side. Old architecture and a quiet street, it's almost unassuming but it still speaks of the kind of wealth that a lot of the established families of New York have. It's on Riverside Drive, which means it's going to have my second gorgeous view of the river today.

We go inside, and unlike my building, Adam's has an elevator. Thank god, I'm so stuffed full of Italian food that I'm not sure I could walk up six flights of stairs right now. I can't help but notice that we're in comfortable silence. That's not typical, at least for me. Most of my silences are awkward. But this feels nice, just existing next to each other without having to fill up the space with words words words.

Adam unlocks the door to the apartment, and…holy shit. It's giant and tastefully decorated in shades of grey and blue, with big windows in the living room, and it's spotless.

My jaw drops. "First, this place is amazing. Second, you told me your place was messy!"

Adam grins, "I told you that to make you feel better. You were freaking out because you thought your apartment was messy."

"It was messy."

"You and I have different ideas about what's messy," he chuckles.

I move further into the living room and look out the windows that overlook the Hudson and Riverside Park. It's so beautiful. And then I turn my attention to the other gorgeous thing in the room: a massive built-in bookshelf with a truly great collection of books. There are quite a few of the same books that I have, and some that I've been wanting to read. And then, I see them. On the top shelf, the entire *World's Waterfall* series.

"Wait a second," I say, pointing. "You've read those?"

Adam smiles, seeming almost embarrassed. "Yeah."

"When?"

He laughs. "I was obsessed with them the same time you were, in high school."

My mind flashes back to that day in the gym when he told me that he hoped I had a chance to finish the book. It was because he loved that book too! "Why didn't you say anything?"

"My father hated them," he says. "He didn't want his kind to be a nerd, or rather, he didn't want a kid that would read those type of books. He wanted someone masculine and smart. Someone who could become a successful doctor.

"In his defense, I think it was at least partially out of love and not ego. He was afraid that I'd be bullied the same way he was, and he didn't want that for me. So I hid my inner nerd and moved on, and it's honestly just become a habit to not talk about it."

I cross the room to him and pull him into a kiss, "I wish I'd known this then," I say. "I wouldn't have been so afraid to talk to you."

"You were *afraid* to talk to me?"

"You were Mr. Popular, and I was very, very not. Of course I was afraid to talk to you."

He laughs. "I'm sorry. Guess we were both freaking out about the same things. I was so nervous to talk to you. I thought you'd blow me off *because* I was popular. But I guess what matters is what we know now, right?"

"Right," I say. "We're both nerds. I'm

glad I know." Suddenly I freeze. "So, at the reunion, I guess that you noticed that—"

"The dress you were wearing is shockingly similar to the one Rienne wears when she and Colbert first have sex? Yeah, I noticed."

I'm really blushing, truly fiery red. "Lor found it and she knew that it was like that dress and she thought it would make me more confident."

Adam pulls back, taking me in. "You don't have to justify why you were wearing it. You looked beautiful. You would have looked beautiful whatever you were wearing. I can't say that it didn't cross my mind though."

"I can't believe that I didn't know." I look back at the bookshelf and suddenly my stomach drops. The books on the shelf are the same kind of gorgeous copies like he gave me, and the first book is missing. "Did you give me your signed copy?"

"Yeah."

Wow. "That's...amazing. But don't you want it?"

"I want you to have it. The copy you have is still the beat up ones from ten years ago."

"Thanks." It was a nice gesture when I thought that he bought it for me. Now that I know it is one of his own books, it feels completely different. Way more intimate and special.

Adam heads towards the kitchen. "Let me grab us some drinks," he says. I think he needs a moment, and I let him go. I keep looking through his bookshelf. I've found that you can tell a lot about a person by which books they do—or don't—read. John Waters famously said, 'If you go home with somebody and they don't have any books, don't fuck 'em.'

Adam, thankfully, seems to have a lot of good books. On the table by the couch I see a copy of the business book that I've been reading. "Did you just buy this?" I ask him as he comes back into the room.

"Yeah, I picked it up on my way home yesterday. What you said about it seemed interesting."

I laugh, and suddenly I can't stop laughing. "I'm sorry, I just can't believe you were actually listening."

311

"Why?" he asks. "Because I happened to be inside you at the time?"

"Yes, that would be why."

He toasts me with his glass and pulls me close to whisper in my ear. "It turns out that I'm a pretty good multi-tasker."

"Oh?" His breath tickles my ear and I laugh, but I lean into him. "You have any plans to multi-task tonight?"

"I might."

"Are you going to tell me?"

"How I'm going to multi-task?"

"Yeah."

He smiles. "I thought I'd surprise you."

I make a face. "I told you before, I don't love surprises."

"Given our particular history," he says, "I get that. I was going to ask if you wanted to watch a movie with me. Then we can make out like the teenage sweethearts that we never got to be." He leads me over to the couch, and I manage to kick off my shoes before I sink onto the couch, careful not to spill my wine.

"Does it need to be a scary movie so I can pretend to be afraid just so that I can have you hold me?"

He laughs, purposely putting his arm around me on the couch. "It can be whatever kind of movie you like."

"Hmmm." I turn so I can see him a little better. "One more question. Does the end of this end up with me in your bed?"

"In many very compromising positions," he says.

"Then bring on the movie," I say, downing the rest of my glass.

Adam turns on the TV, and I tuck my feet up onto the couch, leaning into him. "Now I have two questions for you."

"I might have two answers." I'm feeling the wine from dinner, and with this glass, I'm in perfectly, blissfully tipsy territory. I can tell that I'm smiley, maybe too smiley, but I don't care because I'm happy and I love that I'm here in Adam's apartment and that somehow we're together after all this time doing what we might have done in one or the other of our parents' basements.

"Do you want more wine?"

"Yes."

I feel the vibration of his laughter in his chest. "And do you want to care about the movie?"

"What do you mean?"

He clears his throat. "I mean, do you want a movie that—despite any making out that will happen—we'll want to finish? Or do you want something we can heartlessly abandon halfway through?"

I think about it for a second. "Let's watch the movie," I say. "It's been a long time since I've actually watched a movie with anyone outside a theater. It might be nice."

Adam stands, taking my wine glass. "It will be more than nice," he calls behind him. "It will be excellent." He fills both our glasses

315

and comes back, shrugging off the jacket of his suit before he sits down again. Flicking through movies on the TV, he chooses one that I vaguely remember from the theaters a few months ago, a fluffy romantic comedy that looked funny. "How about this?"

"You really want to watch it?"

"Why not?"

"I don't know," I shrug. "I guess I didn't think this would be your kind of movie."

Adam slides his arm around my waist, settling his hand on my hip. "I don't really have just one kind of movie. I think that any genre can be good if done well."

I take a sip of my wine. "Have I mentioned that I like you?"

"Not today."

"I like you."

He clicks the button on the remote to start the movie. "I like you too."

The story behind the film is pretty simple. There's a girl who's head over heels in love with this guy and they've known each other forever. Only the guy is dating her best friend. And then, they get engaged and suddenly things get twisty when she admits she's still in love with him. It's around that time that I feel Adam stir, and then the soft feeling of lips on my neck.

I'm relaxed and drowsy and tipsy and the sensation of his lips on my skin makes my body wake up and purr. I tilt my head away to give him better access, and he takes it. Teeth

317

graze my skin, and then his lips. I'm not sure we're going to make it to the end of the film.

Reaching over, I set my wine glass down next to his. But when I go to move, to turn so that I can reach him and his lips, the arm around my waist holds me still. "Watch the movie," he says softly.

"How am I supposed to watch when you're doing that?"

His soft laugh makes good chills run across my skin. "Multi-task?"

"Is that what you're doing?" I gasp as he gently bites my shoulder.

He takes my free hand with his and weaves are fingers together, keeping me from reaching for him. "I told you I would."

I try to focus on the plot of the film

while Adam continues his exploration of my neck and shoulder. "Am I showing up to work tomorrow with a hickey?"

"How about you call out sick from work tomorrow and we go straight out to the island?"

I let my head rest back against his shoulder. "As long as you stop and let me grab some stuff from home, I'm yours."

He growls, and moves me so he can reach my neck again. And when there's no more skin that he can reach and hasn't already touched with his mouth, the hand he's been keeping on my waist creeps to my skirt. And then, slowly, underneath it. "Adam," I say.

"Watch the movie."

I try. Turns out the guy had a crush on

the main character and now they're seeing each other behind the back of her best friend and he might break it off with his fiancée. I don't blame them if they're in love but this is a much more serious film than I would have thought. And I keep getting distracted by Adam's fingers, now on my thigh, barely moving but still slowly getting closer.

The anticipation is driving me mad. My breath is shallow and I'm tense, watching the movie and waiting, just waiting for him to touch me. It takes forever. But when he does, fire blooms in my stomach. He moves his fingers under the fabric of my thong so that they're resting on my clit and I can't breathe anymore.

And I still can't breathe, because nothing happens. He doesn't do anything, except for the tiniest of movements to let me know that he's right there. That any moment, he could start to move and give me pleasure and the thought makes me wet. And then I feel the wetness build under his fingers, and blush, the somehow embarrassing and arousing thought that he can *feel* me getting wetter by the second is only making it happen faster.

On the screen, the couple has just been caught together by the best friend and everything is falling apart. Adam's fingers move, just a little, a small circle. I want more, and I reach down to cover his hand with mine, to guide him, but he's faster. His free hand catches me by the wrist and pulls my arm across my body. Now he has both my wrists in his hand, and there's nothing I can do but let him make those small, infuriating movements on my clit.

I twist a little. "What are you doing?"

"Watch the movie," he smirks.

"I can't when you're touching me like that," I say, tensing as he draws another tiny circle.

He makes a face that tells me he's not sorry, that he's amused by my predicament. "You'll survive."

"Adam," I beg. "Please."

"Watch the movie, Olivia." The way he says my name makes me shiver. "Because when it's over, I'm going to take you to bed, and I don't plan on getting very much sleep tonight."

He moves his hand again, harder this

time, and I close my eyes for a second. He's teasing me. Getting me ready for us to play together. I bite my lip and try to focus and ignore the way he's slowly stroking me now as the film comes to a close. The wedding is off, and the best friends don't really make up, but they come to terms. But more importantly, the main character and her man are together and happy and so it's still a happy ending, even if it's a little sad.

But I honestly don't care that much, not when Adam has me hanging on by one twitch of his hand. After what seems like forever, the credits finally roll, and Adam releases my hands to turn off the TV.

"Are you ready?" he asks me.

"For what?" I want him to tell me what he has planned.

He smiles slowly, fingers dipping down to circle my pussy and back up. "To see my bedroom."

CHAPTER TWENTY-ONE

Adam

My cock is so hard that I might pass out because there's not enough blood flowing to my brain. But seeing Ollie worked up like this, biting her lip, panting as I slowly touch her, is well worth it. I guide her off the couch and down the hall to my bedroom, which is my favorite room in my apartment, and really the only one I had any say in decorating. I chose a bed that's so big it takes up easily a quarter of the space. And I'm glad for it now.

The windows in here also look out over the Hudson, and I've got lights that can be set to custom setting. I turn them to a low setting, moody and dark so I can see Ollie but I'm not ruining the mood with bright lights.

She's standing in the middle of the room, looking around at my bedroom, and I try to imagine how she'd see it. But I'm not sure what she's thinking. Finally, "That's an amazing bed."

"I enjoy sleeping in a large one."

"And other things?" She smirks.

I cross back to her. "And other things."

Pulling her back against me, I kiss her neck again. I love this part of her, just like I love every part of her. Her skin is soft under my lips and tongue and I like feeling her react, the way her body tenses and anticipates and yields.

I find her zipper, pull it down, and suddenly the purple dress is a puddle around her feet and she's dressed in nothing but lingerie that's scraps of lace. I didn't think it was possible for me to get any harder. I was wrong.

Ollie looks over her shoulder at me as she walks to my bed and stretches out on it, lifting her ass in the air. Fuck. I can't get my clothes off fast enough. I want to touch her, and I want to be naked when I do. But I don't join her on the bed. I run my hand down her back, cup her ass, and on instinct I take a bite. She makes the most satisfying moan.

"There are so many things that I want to do with you, Ollie."

"Like what?" She's purposely moving her ass under my hand, and I feel like I'm hypnotized.

I draw my hand across her ass, and dare to touch her there. She stills, and I press my finger against her, almost hard enough to enter, but not quite. "Like this."

Ollie turns around, coming to her knees on the bed so we're almost the same height. I hadn't seen her from the front in this underwear, and the deep purple lace is surrounded by straps that look like some kind of sexy web. The thong rides up on her hips and even though it hides nothing, that little piece of fabric makes my cock twitch.

"I've always wanted to try that," she says.

I'm so distracted by the way she looks in lace that I almost don't hear her. "What?"

She smiles slowly. "I said I've always wanted to try that. That and lots of other things."

I suck in a sharp breath. "And how would you feel about trying that tonight?"

Ollie puts her hands around my neck and arches back, and my eyes have no choice but to drop down the line of her perfect, curvy, gorgeous body. "I'm not opposed. I think I'm just drunk enough to try."

I stifle a groan. This wasn't what I had planned. It's way better. Dipping her back further, I cover one of her nipples with my mouth, sucking it through the fabric. "You're going to need a warm-up orgasm," I say, switching to her other breast and listening to her breath speed up.

"That won't take long."

I let her drop back on the bed and for the second time today I get the chance to bury my face in her pussy. I'll never understand men who wouldn't do this. It's pure erotic energy. You can taste just how much a woman wants you, feel her clench down on your tongue and your fingers and nothing feels better than making her come with nothing but your mouth.

Her thong is still there, and I don't bother to remove it. I lick her through the lace, using the friction of the fabric to my advantage. "Oh god," Ollie says. She's already squirming, and I bite down, softly teasing her with it.

I circle her clit with my tongue, over and over. Every time we're together, I learn something about her, and I've already learned that I can lick her to climax if I just keep going, keeping it steady. Ollie pushes the thong down her legs, and I don't stop, helping her pull it off while I seal my mouth over her. I take a second to dip inside her pussy and taste the sweetness there, but only a second. And then I'm back on her clit and loving every second of it.

Ollie's hands are in my hair, pulling me closer, and she's moaning, making the sexiest fucking sound I've ever heard. I can't help the urge, I reach down and stroke my cock, the pleasure the small taste I need to keep myself from coming.

Sealing my mouth over her clit, I suck hard, and Ollie yells. I feel her shake, her pussy surging wetness as she comes. Her body spasms, and I see her hands dig into the sheets. She breathes in sharp gasps, and I can almost see the waves of her orgasm moving through her body. She releases my hair suddenly, and I pull back to see her smiling.

"Was the teasing worth it?"

"Maybe."

"Maybe?" I go to one of my drawers where I keep my condoms and lube and grab them. "Clearly I'll have to do better next time."

Ollie stretches, rolling over onto her stomach, already looking ravished and sated. "You're going to do that again? It almost killed me this time."

"I'll do it until you say that it was absolutely worth it."

She laughs. "We'll see. Maybe we can make a deal."

"What sort of deal?" I ask, crawling onto the bed with her, hauling her against me and kissing her. Fuck, my stomach drops when our lips meet and it feels big. Being with Ollie is better than I could have imagined.

"We'll have to see if you try to tease me," she says. "It'll be a surprise."

"I thought you hated surprises."

She laughs. "Only when I'm the one being surprised."

I grab the condom off the bed. "You're sure about this?"

"Yes." She takes the condom from me and I have to grit my teeth as she rolls it down my cock. I'm so hard that a stiff breeze off the Hudson could make me blow.

She turns over again, and wiggles her ass at me, and I'm just…

"Shit, Ollie."

She giggles, and I grab the lube. I stroke some onto my cock and some onto her ass, and fit myself against her. Stretching out over her, I make sure she can feel me—my chest pressed against her back, my legs on the outside of hers, my cock poised to take her ass. I press, and slowly, I feel her relax, give, and push back. I let up, and push in again. This is going to happen in inches. Millimeters. And I'm going to savor every second.

The tip of my cock slips inside her ass, and holy. Fucking. God.

"Oh," Ollie gasps, tensing beneath me.

"Are you okay?"

"Yeah." Her hands flex on the sheets, gripping and releasing. "It's strange."

I'm having a hard time focusing on her words when her ass is squeezing me like this. "Bad strange?"

"I don't know yet." She relaxes again, and she pushes up into me slightly. "More."

How can I say no to that? I press in further, and shit. My hands are clenched into fists, my jaw tight. I'm sliding inside something so tight, it feels amazing. And even though I already knew, it suddenly hits me that I'm the first person to do this. Ollie's never let anyone do this with her. I'm a first. She trusts me not to hurt her, not to do her harm.

Pressing in another half inch, I groan. "How do you feel?"

"Full," she says, voice airy.

I kiss the skin below her ear. "I'm not even halfway inside you." She moans, and I feel that moan straight in my dick. "Can I keep going?"

She doesn't say anything, but nods. I push in further, and further, slowly sinking into her, and it feels impossible that she's taking this much of me. It shouldn't be possible. But it's happening. Fuck. One of Ollie's hands slips down between her legs and she gasps. She's shaking beneath me, but she doesn't tell me to stop. I move my hips one more time and her ass is touching my stomach.

"Adam," she says, and I don't know what she was going to say.

"Just breathe," I say. I'm not moving yet. Her body's not used to me, and every few seconds she squeezes my cock like she can't believe it's there. Every squeeze makes me go blind with pleasure.

She shudders, and suddenly she jerks, and I go still with shock. "Did you just come?"

"Yes." It's a soft sigh filled with pleasure. "Everything feels...more."

Rocking my hips into her ass, "This feels good?"

"So fucking good."

I move a little more, pulling back and pushing in. Her ass grabs me, holds onto me

337

like it doesn't want to let me go. Fuck. "Ollie," I say, "I need—" My voice is cut off by another squeeze. I'm not going to last much longer, and my muscles are starting to shake from holding myself back, holding myself still.

Ollie tips her hips up and back, pressing her ass into me, and then she's pulling away, pulling herself off of my cock. And then she rolls to her back and spreads her legs, bold, unafraid, eyes filled with lust. She grabs my cock and puts it to her ass. "I want to see you. Take what you need."

Fuck. I grab her hips, thrusting and making it past the barrier with little trouble. Then in and in and in until she's full of me again and I look down to see my cock buried to the hilt in her ass. I fall onto my arms, holding myself above her so we're face to face, and I kiss her. Hard.

She opens for me and I plunge my tongue inside as deep as I can. Her tongue dances with mine, and while I make her dizzy with this kiss, I start to fuck. Slowly at first, and then faster. Short strokes that barely move, growing longer and longer until I'm fucking her full force.

She squeezes down and I can't hold on. I've been too hard for too long and the orgasm explodes through me like nothing I've ever felt before. "Fuck, Ollie!" My voice echoes around the room, and crashing surges of sharp pleasure land on me with every jerk of my cock. I can't see anything, and I'm only aware of Ollie's ass still squeezing me and the fact that my every nerve is fried with pleasure.

"Yes!" Her sudden shout brings my eyes open, and I see Ollie's head thrown back, lips parted in perfect pleasure. She came again. I should have made sure that she did.

I kiss her again, softer this time. The aftermath of pleasure is still zinging through my body in a way that makes me wonder if I'll ever feel the same again. Slowly, I pull out of Ollie and clean myself up before coming back to her. Sudden exhaustion is seeping in, and I'm already fading when I sprawl next to her, my arm across her stomach.

"I know I said that I didn't plan on much sleep…" I say.

Ollie curls towards me, smiling. "I think that was more than either of us planned for."

"Yes. And now I have you for three

more days."

She giggles. "Whatever will we do with ourselves?"

"Off the top of my head," I say, "more of that. More movies. I may want to fuck you on the beach."

"Anything else new you want to try?"

I pull her closer. "You've already been pretty adventurous for a new relationship."

"I want to try everything with you," she says softly.

"Me too," I say, tucking her close to my body. And then there's really nothing left to say, and we fall together into sleep.

CHAPTER TWENTY-TWO

Ollie

The morning I wake up at Adam's apartment is at once a morning of lazy luxury and a whirlwind of activity. Adam wakes me up with kisses and an amazing spread of breakfast that he went out and got, and we almost get carried away before he suggests that we get to the house on the island before we fall into each other again. It's not easy to stop.

I call into work and say that I won't be there. There's nothing terribly urgent at the office that I need to take care of this week anyway. And then Adam zips me back into the purple dress and I make the walk of shame with him in a cab to my apartment. It's weird being out in this dress so early in the morning, but I honestly don't feel ashamed about it at all. Though I'll be happy to throw on some jeans.

Once we get to my apartment, I pack the fastest I've ever packed in my life, grabbing cosmetics and a couple of dresses and my bathing suits. I'm not going to kid myself and pretend like I'll be wearing clothes a lot. We both know that's not going to happen.

Adam calls another car, a different service, and we pile into the back of a big black SUV and we're driving. It's a far drive, and even though I try, I'm almost lulled into sleep leaning on Adam. We were up late, and I'm still tired. I can't believe that I did that. I'm very glad that I did, but thank god I was tipsy enough to let him go there. If I'd been sober, the embarrassment of him even suggesting anal sex would have made me say no.

I really didn't anticipate how good it would feel. The orgasms I had weren't explosive. They were *deep*. They slithered down into my bones and made me shake. It was a completely different kind of pleasure, like Adam fucking my ass turned on nerves that I never knew I had. I guess I shouldn't be surprised. If I can come from him touching my nipples, my body is clearly wired differently.

Suddenly I jerk awake. I hadn't realized

I was fully asleep until the car stopped. "We're here," Adam says.

I look outside the car and—holy shit. "Adam, how rich is your family?"

"Richer than we let on," he says.

He helps me out of the car and grabs our bags before paying the driver. In front of us is a house. He called it a house. It's not a house, it's a fucking mansion is what it is. And not only that, it's on the beach. I can see the water stretching to infinity behind the house and I'm pretty sure that I still haven't picked up my jaw from where it's fallen to the ground.

"Why isn't your family here all the time?"

Adam laughs. "Neither of my parents

actually *like*s the beach that much. They mostly came out for the parties that their friends were having, but all their friends prefer the city now too. It's empty most of the time."

"Wow."

There's a keypad that looks like part of a security system that's no joke, and Adam enters the code to let us inside. It's like walking into a house that's been a movie set. It's gorgeous and modern, but it also looks like it's never been used. Like it was set up just for us.

The foyer reaches straight through the house to where there are sets of French doors opening onto a gorgeous patio and then the beach. Stairs wind up and out of sight, and I can see glimpses of the kitchen through the living room to the right. "This is amazing."

"What do you want to do first?"

I open my mouth to say something and close it. More than once. "I don't even know where to start."

"How about a swim?" Adam asks.

Glancing through the house toward the ocean, it does look really inviting. "That sounds nice."

We go upstairs, Adam carrying the bags, and we go into a bedroom that's bigger than my entire apartment, and I don't even think that's an exaggeration. "This is the master," Adam says, giving me a look. "It has the biggest bed."

"Obviously the most important part," I say, grabbing my suitcase and pulling out one of the bikinis I packed. It's black and purple and I've never worn it because it's just a tad too small. I've never been in a situation that I've been comfortable enough to wear it in. But I think today is the day. "Is the beach public?"

Adam shakes his head. "Occupants only. We might see some neighbors, but I doubt it." He puts on a pair of swim trunks, and I'm distracted by the way the lines on his hips slip down into his trunks and he catches me staring. "Of course," he says, "we don't *have* to go for a swim."

"Let's go," I say too quickly.

Adam grabs towels for us, and the minute I step out the back door I realize just how much I've missed the beach. I can't remember the last time I've actually been. New York will do that to you. You always talk

348

about the things that you want to do, but you get so busy that you never actually do them. The air is breezy and has that salt smell that I would love to bottle and inhale every day. Every second. I close my eyes to breathe it in, and when I open them I find Adam staring at me. "What?"

"You look different," he says softly.

"I love the beach," I say. "It's the closest I have to a happy place."

"Why?"

I think, but nothing comes to mind. "I don't know, really. I just…we—my family—we'd always go on vacation to the beach. And it was just happy. Whenever I think about the beach I feel happy. It stuck."

"I'm glad." Adam drops the towels on

the sand. "Does that happiness include what's about to happen?"

"What's about to happen."

"I'm going to dunk you in the ocean." He scoops me off my feet and over his shoulder.

I scream, startled and happy, "Adam!" He jogs with me towards the water, and then he's in it and my feet get splashed. "It's cold!"

"Yes, it is." And then he's up to his waist and we go down together. I'm plunged into freezing cold and it hurts and it feels amazing and I don't remember when I've felt this alive. I come up gasping for air and soaking, Adam right next to me. The sun is reflecting off his now wet body and oh my god he's breathtaking. Just looking at him gives me a twinge in my chest, and I didn't realize it before, but holy shit I am in trouble.

I knew I liked him. I knew I was having fun. I didn't know that it might be more. That I might be falling head over heels for him in a way that could be amazing or disastrous. But that moment is gone, because Adam has a wolfish grin on his face, and he tackles me into the water. I manage to shriek only a second before we go under again.

Time seems to pass in a blur, and it's a passing thought that we're once again a cliché —playing in the waves on the beach. But it's nice, and after an hour I'm exhausted. I stumble up the sand and spread my towel before collapsing onto it. "You've worn me out," I say to Adam as he sits next to me.

"I hope not," he says. "I have plans for

later."

"Yeah? What plans?"

He stretches out, arms behind his head. "We could have a fire on the beach, watch another movie, go out to dinner. Oh, and all the sex."

I laugh. "You're insatiable."

"For you I am."

We sit for a while, catching our breath and resting. I keep turning over so that I don't burn. You would have thought that knowing we were coming to the beach that I would remember sunscreen, but I didn't.

When we go inside, I'm starving. We haven't eaten since breakfast, and it's well into the afternoon now. Adam calls out for some delivery while I take a quick shower and change into the comfy clothes I brought: sweats and an oversized sweater that has a bad habit of slipping off my shoulders. I'd never admit to Adam that that's why I brought it, to tease him, but that's why.

And then we curl up together on the couch, and soon my head is in his lap, and I'm dozing off while we watch a movie. An action film this time that's fast and colorful and it doesn't really matter what the plot is as long as there are lots of explosions.

I can't remember the last time I was this relaxed. Everything is perfect, and even though I feel like I've been falling asleep all day, I'm so close to slipping under. Adam is stroking my hair, his other hand settled on my hip, and I think as I'm fading, that this is perfect happiness.

When I wake up the sun is setting and Adam isn't on the couch with me. I sit up and I see him in the kitchen, the beeps of the microwave faint. "Hi," I say.

"I didn't want to wake you," he says. "There's pizza."

My stomach growls at the mention of food. I was already hungry earlier and I fell asleep before it even got here. "Yes, please."

He sets a plate of food in front of me as I make my way to the breakfast bar. My sweater slips off my shoulder and I don't fix it. I notice the way Adam glances at my suddenly bare skin and stifle a grin. I guess I was right on when bringing this sweater. "Did you finish the movie?" I'm wolfing down the pizza in a way that's probably really unsexy, but I don't care because it's really good. And I immediately feel more awake, like I've given myself a shot of caffeine.

"I did. The good guys won."

I lift my fist in the air. "Go good guys."

He laughs. "I thought that maybe we'd do the fire tomorrow?"

"Fine with me. What now then?"

"Well…" There's a wild and feral gleam in his eyes that I recognize. He comes around the counter and spins my stool so that he's standing between my legs. "I had another idea, if you're open to a little adventurous experimentation."

I raise an eyebrow. "Oh?"

"Do you remember our little video chat?"

Of course I do, and I immediately blush because somehow it's still embarrassing. "Yes."

Adam runs his hands down my sides, and they cup my ass, pulling me closer on the stool. "I told you that I loved your tits, and that I wanted to fuck them till we both came."

My stomach drops with desire, my pussy going instantly slick. I turn away from him, grabbing the rest of my pizza and finishing in several huge bites. "Yes," I say. "Yes."

I don't wait for him, hopping off the stool and going upstairs. I know he's going to follow me. I walk into our bedroom, stripping as I go. I stretch out on the bed and savor the look on Adam's face when he walks in and sees me posed and waiting.

Watching Adam pull his shirt over his head is like watching a work of art. I could play it on repeat forever. And that's just the prelude to what comes next. Watching him step out of his shorts is an entirely different kind of art and it makes my mouth water. He only pauses on the way to the bed to grab a bottle of lotion from his bag. "You came prepared."

"Yes, I did." He takes my mouth in a kiss before settling his knees on either side of my waist. His cock is so close, and the way he's towering over me is overwhelming. But he doesn't do what I expect. He doesn't jump in. Instead, he takes the bottle of lotion and squeezes some into his hands. And then he touches me. I don't know if I'll ever get used to the way that it affects me, like it sinks through my skin and drops down to my core and brings my arousal to the surface.

Adam slowly massages my breasts, moving them together and apart and together again, thumbs slowly rubbing across my nipples. I groan, because this feels so good. At once relaxing and hot and I swear to god it's like he's touching my pussy. My nipples harden under his fingers and I squirm, the urge to touch myself strong, to get there faster and we've only just started.

He's making eye contact with me, and I can't look away. It's not awkward the way I thought it might be. It's so damn sexy that I can't breathe. Adam pushes my breasts together again and thrusts his cock into the space between them. Oh my god. The slickness of the lotion on my skin and the hardness of his cock send fireworks shooting through my chest and down to my clit.

He presses them harder together, fingers slipping on my skin as he thrusts again, and again. No other man I've been with would believe me when I told them that this feels like getting fucked, but it does. My pussy is so wet it's dripping and if I touched my clit right now, I'm sure I'd come.

Adam's eyes close and I reach up and put my hands on his, pressing harder. He lets me, falling onto his hands, and thrusting harder, faster. It takes my breath away and the pleasure building behind my clit is spreading.

Like I'm slowly wading into an ocean of it. I want more, more, more.

I push so hard it almost hurts, until I can feel every ridge and vein as he slips between my skin. Adam is grunting with the effort of every thrust, and I see his face. It's caught in a storm of pleasure, fierce and taut, and oh—

The wave breaks before I expect and now I'm caught in my own storm of pleasure. It writhes through me, and I'm quaking, coming, every breath deeper.

Adam breathes out sharply, thrusting once more, and I feel the heat of his cum on my skin, wave after wave of it. And I'm still feeling the aftershocks of my own. We're both frozen and breathing together, and I'm so glad that I can come like this. That I feel safe enough with Adam to try stuff like this.

When he finally slides off me, Adam goes to grab a towel. I think he's about to help me clean up, but then he stops. "We could shower instead."

"Together?"

"Of course."

I'm off the bed before he finishes the words and he has to race to catch up with me.

CHAPTER TWENTY-THREE

Ollie

I wake up to a slamming sound.

"Adam!"

It's a distinctly male voice, and one that I don't remember. Somebody is in the house. I'm hazy as I come to consciousness, covered in nothing but a sheet. I'm definitely naked. I flip over to find Adam just as blearily coming awake. The bedroom is a mess, blankets and pillows everywhere. He and I could have written a sex manual with everything that we did last night, and my body is sore and sated enough to prove it.

"Adam," the voice calls again, booming

and angry. "I know you're here. Get your ass down here, now."

I watch his face go pale as he rolls out of bed and grabs his pants off the floor. He goes straight out of the room, and immediately I hear yelling. "What the hell are you doing?" The voice says. I'm assuming that it's Adam's dad. Though why he's here and why he's yelling are the things I'm unclear on.

I grab my comfy clothes from where I left them on the floor and put them on. Creeping to the door, I listen. I would try not to, but Adam's father isn't exactly keeping his voice down.

"I get a call from Dr. Pratt saying you took days off, and then I get a call from Sasha telling me that she hasn't heard from you in days. Is this how you treat the mother of your

363

child? You should be talking with her every single day and making sure she's okay. A healthy relationship means a healthy baby."

I feel like a bucket of ice has been dumped on me. Dr. Pratt. Sasha. *Sasha Pratt.* Sasha from high school and prom. Adam has a *baby* with her?

Adam is speaking now, fast and low, and I can't hear what he's saying. Screw staying out of sight now, I walk out onto the landing, and immediately his father's eyes are on me. Adam whips around, seeing me at the stop of the stairs. "Is that true?" I ask. "You got Sasha pregnant."

"You're sneaking off to be with *her*?" his father hisses. "Adam, this is unacceptable on every level. End this now. Come home and take care of Sasha. It's the very least you can do not to be a total disgrace." The look that he gives me makes me feel like I'm about an inch tall, and the hatred pulsing off him is palpable. He turns and stalks to the door, turning around at the last second. "I came all the way out here because I hoped that I was wrong. I hoped that you weren't a complete disappointment. I was wrong."

He leaves, slamming the door behind him and taking all the oxygen with him.

Adam turns to me, and takes a deep breath. I cut him off. "What the fuck is he talking about, Adam? This entire time you've been with Sasha and you have a baby? Never mind the fact that it's Sasha, you didn't think you should tell me that you're with someone else?" The words feel like they're cutting me as I speak them. Bullets and glass shards shredding the happiness I had not even twelve hours ago.

"It's not what you think," he says, coming up the stairs.

"Oh really."

"It's not," he says carefully. "Please let me explain."

I backtrack into the bedroom and grab my bag. "You have five minutes."

He sighs, rubbing his hand over his face. "Dr. Pratt is my boss. My dad thought it would be a good idea for me to date Sasha so that he would like me. This was years ago now, and I went along with it because I thought it would help my career. I've never slept with Sasha and made it clear that I never will. She's convinced that we'll be together

366

eventually even though I've told her no a thousand times. Please, don't go."

I keep gathering my things, though there aren't many things to gather. "If you didn't want to be with her then why not just break it off?"

"Because I'm an idiot," he says. "That's the real answer. But I was too busy with residency and I liked the attention that Dr. Pratt gave me. Since I wasn't focused on having a girlfriend, I didn't care that I had a fake one that much. Sasha liked to tell people that she was dating a doctor. Until about a week ago, I thought that it wasn't hurting anybody.

"But then the reunion happened. That brunch I had to go to, Sasha and her father were there. She cornered me alone, and she'd seen us together. I told her I wanted to break it off, and she freaked out." Adam's voice is uneven now, and he's starting to pace. "She told me no, and I didn't care. I went back to our table fully prepared to break the news, and Sasha came with me. She told our fathers that she was pregnant, and then she told me that she would provide proof that I had cheated on every residency exam. That she would ruin my career if I didn't go along with it. I didn't know what to do. I still don't."

I feel like I'm being slowly ripped to shreds. "Why didn't you tell me?"

"How? How could I tell you that I'd been 'with' the girl that had tried to ruin your life? Who hated you? I honestly didn't know I would ever see you again, Ollie. If I'd known, I never would have done this. It's the worst decision I've ever made."

I clear my throat. "Why didn't you tell me? If the baby is fake, why were you so worried? You thought I wouldn't believe you?"

He sinks down onto the edge of the bed, saying nothing.

"Adam?"

"I don't know."

I grab my bag, "You lied to me. Not only did you lie to my face the entire time, you lied to me about *her*."

"I was going to tell you, Ollie. I was, I just didn't know how. I was trying to figure a way out, to try to figure out how to counter blackmail. Sasha knows everybody, and she doesn't bluff. I didn't want to lose my career or you." He stands, coming to me, but he makes the wise decision not to try to touch me. "I had just found you, and I didn't want to break your heart. Not when it seemed like we had a chance to heal it together."

Tears spring into my eyes and I have to turn away. I start heading toward the door and I hear his footsteps follow me. "It's a little late for that, Adam."

"Please don't go, Ollie." He says. "I promise there's nothing between Sasha and me. We've never even kissed. There's nothing."

I don't answer. I can't stay here. This whole thing was a lie or a sham or a ruse and I don't know which, and I like him too much to let him try to comfort me. Because if he tries to comfort me, there's a chance that I'll forgive him. And I can't. There's too much history for that right now. I can't be here.

I slam the door behind me and call a cab, waiting at the end of the driveway until it comes. Adam watches me from the doorway until I disappear.

***

Lorraine shows up with ice cream and coffee and tissues. I don't have to let her in, she still has her key. I didn't call her yesterday. I didn't do anything yesterday except come home and cry. Of all the people, why Sasha? It might be irrational, though I'm not sure, but it seems like I'm relieving high school all over again. Everyone is staring and laughing at me. Somehow, ten years later, this is happening again. I've been had. Fooled.

I'm on the floor in front of the couch wrapped in a blanket when Lorraine comes in. "What the fuck?" she asks me. I didn't tell her much—just the gist. That Adam's been lying and we may have broken up. Even though we hadn't had the conversation about whether or not we were officially together. But we were. I know we were.

She hands me the coffee and disappears to put the ice cream in the freezer before kicking off her shoes and plopping down next to me. "Spill."

And that's all it takes to get me crying again. Somehow I manage to get it all out. The coffee does make me feel better, and I manage to stem the tears by the time I fill her in on everything that he said. "Do I believe him?"

I'm actually asking.

Lor takes a sip of her coffee, and I recognize the deep in thought look on her face. "First, he's an asshole for lying to you."

"Yes."

"Second, he's a particular kind of asshole for lying about Sasha Pratt."

"Yes."

She clears her throat. "But, you never knew the Carlisles in high school. I did. There were get-togethers with the sports teams and the cheerleaders at their house sometimes. And I know that Mr. Carlisle is a fucking piece of work. He's a heartless workaholic who would do absolutely anything to advance his career. Or his son's. So the idea that he would tell Adam to date her for that reason makes absolute sense."

"Yeah," I say, "I got a sense of his piece of work when he showed up."

"And didn't you say that Adam told you the whole reason Sasha pulled that stunt at prom was because he turned her down?"

I nod.

"I know that it happens and people change their minds," she says, "but I think I believe him when he says that they're not really together."

"Why?"

"Because, like I said at the reunion, people like Sasha don't change. And if she's creating a fake baby, it's clear that her particular brand of crazy hasn't exactly disappeared in the last ten years."

"Yeah." I let my head fall back against the couch. "I don't know what to do. Why does it feel like this?"

"Like what?"

I huff a laugh. "Like my chest is cracking open and everything is leaking out onto the floor."

"Oh, that." She toasts me with her coffee. "That's because you're in love with him."

"What?" I'm frozen.

"Seriously?" Lor asks. "You can't be surprised by this."

I shake my head. "I'm not in love with Adam."

"If you weren't," she says, "then this would hurt less. You would get over the pain and move on if it were just a fling. But you're not going to be over this tomorrow."

That feeling when we were playing in the water. That's what it was. I thought I might be falling, but I missed the fact that I was already there. "What do I do, Lor?"

"I don't know."

"That's not your real answer."

She sighs. "It sucks, what he did, and he was a real dick not to tell you, but I also can see why. Like, if I'd gone into a career that took seven years of school, I'd want to protect it. And Sasha...is a force of nature. She's crazy, she's rich, and apparently she's got it in her head that Adam is hers. I think he's right to be afraid of her."

I nod, taking another sip of coffee and throwing the blanket off my legs. "That still doesn't tell me what to do."

"I'm not going to tell you what to do."

"Why not?" I whine.

She rolls her eyes. "Because I'm not your mother. But I do have an idea, and you can decide."

"Hit me."

"He invited you to that party tomorrow, right?"

I wave a hand. "Yeah, it's at his parents' house."

"So go."

"Are you serious? That's insane."

"It's not." She's got her game face on. "You know he's going to be there. If you decide that you can forgive him, you can talk to him and show him that you can handle being with the type of crowd that his family hangs out with. If you want revenge, you can tell everyone at the party what he did."

That thought makes me sick to my stomach. "That would be like pulling a prom night on him. I don't think I could do that."

"Well, then maybe you going can give him the opportunity to get out from under Sasha, even if you guys don't end up together."

"I don't know."

Lor grins. "I'll crash with you. I've still got some great dresses for us. Backups from the reunion."

I look at her. "You're not going to stop until I say I'm going to go, are you?"

"Nope."

"Fine."

She's right. This is a good solution for now. All I have to do is figure out what I want to do before tomorrow night.

CHAPTER TWENTY-FOUR

Ollie

"This is a stupid idea."

Lor laughs. "This is a brilliant idea and we look fabulous."

No matter if Lor has worked her magic —and she has by putting me in an emerald green dress that women would kill for—it's still a stupid idea. I'm more nervous about this than I was about walking into the reunion. I suppose that's because there was a chance of being tortured at the reunion, and when I walk into this party, there's an almost absolute chance of some kind of scene.

Adam had already given me the address

to his parents' sprawling brownstone on the Upper East Side, and now I'm standing outside hyperventilating. Lorraine grabs my arm. "We can't just stand outside in these clothes. We need to go in. It will be fine. Breathe."

We go up the steps together and the door opens. The butler doesn't ask to see an invitation, this isn't that kind of party. Thanks to Lor's brilliant work, our clothes are all the invitation we need. "I'll be at the bar, waiting. If you need a drink, come find me."

"I will definitely need a drink," I mutter under my breath, but she's already gone.

My plan is to find Adam first. I want to hear it from him again that it's not true, that Sasha isn't pregnant and that they're not together. I want him to look me in the eyes and tell me the truth, again. Then we can talk about dealing with Sasha. I move as quickly as I can through the rooms—I need to find him quickly before someone realizes that I'm really not supposed to be here.

I make it once around the party and am starting my second circuit when I hear a voice to my right. Loud, brassy, and completely recognizable. "What the hell are *you* doing here?"

Sasha.

I turn, and give her the least antagonizing smile I can. "I need to speak to Adam. Have you seen him?"

"Of course I have," she says loudly, drawing the eyes of those around us. "He's my boyfriend. And the father of my child. I'm not going to tell you where he is, you stalker."

I jerk back. "What?"

"You've been stalking him for ten years. You wanted him in high school, and ever since that reunion you've been following him everywhere. To his job, even to his family's house on the island. It's sad, Olivia. You need to stop. You're dangerous, and you disgust me."

I close my eyes, fighting flashbacks of Sasha playing the victim at prom and everyone chanting cheater. I keep my voice calm and level—there's no way getting upset is going to help me in this situation. "Sasha, I'm not stalking Adam, he invited me. I just need to speak with him for five minutes, and I'll be on my way."

People are staring now, some starting to move in, drawn to the conflict like a flame. I flex my hands, trying to calm my nerves. Where is Adam?

Sasha looks around and sees the people that are watching us. Suddenly, she flinches away from me, taking several large steps back, cradling her stomach protectively. "You stay away from me, Olivia! Please, don't hurt me or my baby. You need help, and we'll get you some. We know you used to hurt yourself and that you're upset but please don't hurt me!"

My jaw drops. "What on earth are you talking about? Why would I ever want to hurt you?"

Suddenly Adam and his father appear in the doorway. Adam's face is a journey of emotion: shock and hope and pain and what I hope is relief. His father is the opposite, a face of mask of fury. He storms across the floor and pulls Sasha further away from me. "For the sake of the baby, Sasha, stay away from that woman."

I still don't understand what's happening, "What? I don't—"

He cuts me off. "I won't have my grandchild around someone with a history of violence and attempted suicide."

Blood rushes to my face, and Adam is suddenly by my side. I don't understand. I've never hurt anyone. Never tried to kill myself. I've never even thought about killing myself. And if I had, I don't think treating me like this would be the answer.

His father continues. "Don't deny it.

It's well known that you went off the deep end ten years ago. Became so depressed you attacked your friends and then slit your wrists."

My wrists. At the reunion. I look at Adam. "Is that why you were look at my wrists? You thought I tried to kill myself?"

"I'd heard the rumor," he says softly.

I fight the tears making their way to my eyes. "So you were checking to see if I'd gone crazy?"

"Never," he says. The truth in that word runs bone deep. "I wasn't trying to judge you, or avoid you. I wanted to make sure you were okay."

I look across the room, and no one is looking at Sasha. But she's looking at me, and there's a tiny, vindictive smile on her face. It clicks. She's the one that started the rumor. She knew that Adam hadn't been turned against me by her stunt at prom and she needed a way to make sure he didn't come after me. It's truly ironic that she's calling me a stalker—she's been after Adam for ten years.

"Adam," his father says, voice thundering. "We've spoken about this. You need to take care of Sasha and the baby. Not spend your time catering to a suicidal whore," he spits.

I feel like I've been stabbed in the gut, and Adam steps in front of me. "There is *NO BABY!*" His voice echoes through the house and the entire party goes so silent you can hear the traffic outside. "There never was." He points at Sasha. "She made it up. In fact, the whole thing was made up. You're the one who pushed us together in the first place to make a good impression on Dr. Pratt, and somewhere along the way you forgot that it wasn't real."

His father starts to bluster, but Adam doesn't let him speak. "Make her take a pregnancy test right now. We've never slept together. She is not pregnant. We are not a couple. She made up the baby as a way to blackmail me into staying in this fake relationship, and I'm done." He looks at Sasha. "We're *done*. Try to ruin me or not, I don't care, I can't do this. And yes, it's my fault that we lied for so long. I got too deep, and I was stupid for not coming clean sooner. But I need to be honest now."

He turns to me and takes my hands. "I

love you." There's a soft gasp from the room. "I want to be with you, and I'm sorry that I lied to you. I'll never do it again." He kisses me softly, and I let him. How can I not? His next words are soft enough that only I can hear. "I don't care if I lose my career, I'll find another one. I choose you."

I kiss him this time, and I can almost forget that we're in the middle of the party except, "Are you kidding me?!" Sasha is shrieking at the top of her lungs. She looks at Mr. Carlisle, "You're just going to let him abandon me and our—"

"Sasha." A deep voice cuts across the room, and a man with silver hair and an impeccable suit steps into view. "That's enough."

Adam wraps his arms around me,

keeping me pressed against his body, but he doesn't feel tense.

"Daddy—"

"No," he says, and I realize that this must be Dr. Pratt.

He approaches Adam and me, and I blush under his gaze. He looks at the two of us long and hard, and then he speaks. But not to the room, just to us. "I wish I had known. Adam, I'm sorry that you felt the need to keep this from me, or that you ever felt you needed to boost your approval by dating my daughter. You're a fine doctor, and I don't need you to date Sasha in order to tell you that."

"Thank you, Sir."

"It's nice to meet you, Olivia," he says.

"I hope to see you at the hospital soon."

Adam pulls me tighter. "You will," he answers for me.

Dr. Pratt turns back to the room. "Sasha, you and I are going home. It seems we have a lot to talk about."

She sulks and glares at Adam and me, but amazingly, she goes. The room erupts into whispers as soon as they leave, and I duck my head into Adam's chest. There's nothing I want to do right now but hide. Even though the fight is over, everyone is still watching.

Lor appears with a drink in her hand. "That was *epic*," she gushes, "but maybe we should let people get back to the party."

"More like gossip," Adam mutters. "But yes, let's go."

391

His father is still glaring at us as we leave.

As soon as we're out of the house, Lorraine hails a cab. "Have fun, you two!"

"Do you want to go with her?" Adam asks softly.

I shake my head. "No." I don't want to let go of his hand.

"In that case, my place or yours?"

"Yours is closer."

He nods in agreement and hails a cab. We don't speak on the cab ride, though are hands are locked together. It somehow feels wrong to talk about what we need to talk about in a cab. So we wait until we get to his apartment. He goes around turning on lights, and I go to the windows and watch the streetlights from New Jersey sparkle on the river.

"Ollie," Adam says, appearing behind me. He wraps his arms around my waist, and I lean back into him. "I'm sorry."

"I know," I say. My mind has been racing since we left the party, and I'm still not all the way there. "I came to the party to talk to you, not to fight with her. I want you to know that."

"I know. And I'm sorry that it happened. I'm sorry for so much."

I turn around in the circle of his arms, and drape mine around his neck. "I accept your apology. I'm still hurt by the fact that you lied, but I can understand why you did. That isn't going to stop me from kicking your ass if you ever lie to me again."

"I fully expect you to."

I clear my throat and look away. "But can I ask you something?"

"Anything."

"You said that you—"

"I love you," he finishes. "Yes, I love you."

Warmth spreads through my body, a perfect glow surrounding me. "You love me."

"I do."

I lean my head on his chest. "I love you too."

He tugs on my hair, guiding my face up until he can reach my lips and he kisses me, hard and desperate and so sweet it takes my breath away. "Let me take you to bed, Olivia Mitchell, and show you in many ways how thoroughly I love you."

I laugh, the sound freeing, and Adam sweeps me off my feet and into his arms and into his bedroom. Maybe *our* bedroom at some point in the future. I can't wait to find out.

EPILOGUE

Adam

<u>One Year Later</u>

I carry both of the drinks down onto the sand, and hand the one with zero alcohol in it to my very pregnant wife. My wife. It still hasn't been quite long enough for me not to be enamored of the title. She's currently cradled in a beach chair with a book propped on her belly and a floppy sun hat covering most of her face. She looks up as I approach. "Hey, handsome."

"Hello there, beautiful."

She snorts. "I'm a whale."

I hand her the iced tea that she asked for and take a sip of my beer. We decided to take a baby moon before the little one arrives. Still a couple months to go, so we came to the beach. A small house with a very private beach.

It's the perfect time for it. My residency just finished and I have a few months before I start my work as a pediatrician. I'm staying at Columbia under Dr. Pratt, who never once doubted me or my integrity even after everything that happened with Sasha. I think he's almost more excited about the baby than I am, and that's saying a lot because I'm so excited to be a father that I haven't been able to keep a smile off my face in months.

"You are not a whale," I say. "And if you are, you're the hottest whale I've ever seen."

Ollie rolls her eyes but I'm not kidding. I love everything about the way she looks, from the way her breasts have gotten bigger to the curves of her belly. My wife is fucking sexy, and it's a struggle not to get hard whenever I'm within a ten-foot radius.

"I've got another one," I say, and I can almost hear Olivia roll her eyes. She pretends she's not amused by my bad baby name suggestions, but she is.

"Hit me."

"Chrysanthemum."

Ollie bursts out laughing. "We are not naming our daughter Chrysanthemum."

"We could."

"We're *not*." But she's laughing. "If

we're going with flowers I still like Lily or Rose."

"What about Aqua?"

"Adam," she warns.

"Turquoise. Lavender."

She takes a sip of the iced tea I brought her. "You're ridiculous."

"And you love me."

"I do," she says, shifting in her seat in an attempt to get more comfortable.

"How's the book?"

She sighs. "It's okay."

"You a little bored?"

"Yeah."

I reach out and grab her hands, help her to her feet. "Come on."

She smiles. "Where are we going?"

"In the water," I say.

Ollie loves the water, and every time she steps into the ocean she lights up like a Christmas tree. Plus, I know that floating makes her feel better for a bit, carrying the baby. But to my surprise, she shakes her head with a coy smile. "Not right now."

"Oh?"

"I think I'd like a nap."

I struggle to keep the smirk off my face as I help her gather her things off the sand. "A nap, you say?" I carry everything for her as I follow her into the house. She's carrying more than enough—she's carrying our baby girl. Holding the door open for her, I make sure she gets up the stairs and into the house without trouble.

She sighs and steps in the kitchen. "A nap." She grabs an apple and takes a bite.

"You know that a nap takes place in a bed?"

She snorts. "Yeah, usually."

Reaching out, I grab her ass and pull her close. "There are other things that we can do in a bed."

Ollie sighs, and sets down her book on the counter. I know that the sigh doesn't have to do with me suggesting sex. It's that she doesn't feel sexy, and isn't convinced that I still want her that way. I've been doing my best to prove her wrong. I walk with her to the bedroom, never not touching her. I catch her before she lies down, holding her to me and cradling her belly with my hands. "Ollie, let me love you."

"Only if you really want to."

"Can you feel how much I want to?" I'm hard as a rock, and I push my hips forward to make sure she feels it.

I peek around to see what she's thinking, and she's blushing. I help her onto the bed, and before she can make another excuse, I put myself over her. "Olivia, look at me."

She does, even though I can tell she's embarrassed. She embarrasses easily, and sometimes it's cute. Sometimes it turns her on. And sometimes it traps her in her own head until she can't think. This is one of those times. "You're the sexiest woman I know."

I untie the straps of her bikini and reveal her breasts. I kiss one and then the other, but I don't play with them. Not now. That's not what she needs. Instead I lay behind her, removing her bikini bottom. "You're sexy all the time," I whisper in her ear, "*Especially* when you're carrying my baby."

I kick my shorts off and fit my body against hers so that we're touching everywhere. I lift one of her legs over mine and thrust into her in one go, making her gasp. She's wet, and I grin against her neck. "I knew you were in the mood."

"I'm always in the mood for you," she breathes.

Her pussy is hot and slick and god she feels good. She always feels good, and I can never get enough. I'd spend every second of my life in bed with this woman if I could. It feels even better since we haven't had sex in a while. "Ollie, wife, feel free to take advantage of me at any time."

I can see her blush, but I thrust deeper and her head falls back in a silent cry. Good. Reaching around, I tease her clit, running my fingers across the slickness of her skin and teasing the circles I know that drive her crazy. "Or," I say, "if that makes you feel weird, I'll make you a deal."

"What deal?" Her voice is mostly moan, and I realize just how much she wanted this. She's close already.

"Three orgasms a day until the baby comes," I say, "though I reserve the right to give you more. That way you don't have to ask, and I get the distinct pleasure of seeing you come often."

I drive into her harder, and she moans, her pussy crushing down on my cock like a vice. She comes, panting little breaths, and reaching back to grab at me, pull me closer. I let her, but I don't stop fucking her. "That was one."

I let my hand slide across her clit again, stroking up and down and around, up and down and around, she sinks into me, her orgasm passing and I graze my teeth on her shoulder. She tenses suddenly, "Oh god, fuck, Adam," She comes again, and this time I feel the gush of wetness from her, and she moans as I speed up my fingers and their pattern. "That was two," I say, gripping her hips and letting myself go. The more we've played, the more I've discovered that Ollie likes to be fucked hard. She's never asked me to pull back or slow down. I drive myself into her, deep as I can, the sound of me slamming into her loud and mixing with the way she's saying my name.

God I'm close. I close my eyes and listen to her, the way her voice makes my name sound like the most erotic word on earth sends me over, and I yell out my orgasm. I spill myself deep inside her pussy, warmth surrounding my cock as I feel the waves crash through me. Ollie is still shaking, she never really stopped coming after the second orgasm, and now we're lying, panting together.

"That was only two," she says, turning over slowly to look at me.

I pull her close and kiss her. "I never

said I would give you them all at the same time. Gives us both something to look forward to."

She giggles, face still flushed with pleasure, and I swear to god that I'm the luckiest man alive. "I think I'm going to like this deal."

"Me too." I kiss her again, soft and slow, and I love the way her body relaxes, all the tension leaving as I press her back into the pillows. "Have a good nap, wife. I love you."

"I love you too."

THE END

Author Biography

Penny Wylder writes just that-- wild romances. Happily Ever Afters are always better when they're a little dirty, so if you're looking for a page turner that will make you feel naughty in all the right places, jump right in and leave your panties at the door!

<u>Other Books by Penny Wylder</u>

Filthy Boss

Her Dad's Friend

Rockstars F#*k Harder

The Virgin Intern

Her Dirty Professor

The Pool Boy

Get Me Off

Caught Together

Selling Out to the Billionaire

Falling for the Babysitter

Lip Service

Full Service

Expert Service

The Billionaire's Virgin

The Billionaire's Secret Babies

Her Best Friend's Dad

Own Me

The Billionaire's Gamble

Seven Days With Her Boss

Virgin in the Middle

The Virgin Promise

First and Last

Tease

Spread

Bang

Second Chance Stepbrother

Dirty Promise

Sext

Quickie

Bed Shaker

Deep in You

The Billionaire's Toy

Buying the Bride

Dating My Friend's Daughter

Perfect Boss

The Roommate's Baby

Cowboy Husband

FLIRT

LUST

CLAIM

Made in the USA
San Bernardino, CA
02 November 2018